Dry Land Tourist

Canadian Cataloguing in Publication Data

Maguire, Elizabeth Dianne Rose Kelvin, 1947 -
Dry Land Tourist

ISBN 0-920813-67-4

1. Jamaica - Social conditions - Fiction
I. Title.

PS8576.A48D7 1991   C813'.54   C91-095002-4
PR9199.3.M34D7 1991

Illustrations: Dianne Maguire
Consulting editor: Ramabai Espinet
Printed and bound in Canada by union labour

Published by: **Sister Vision Press**
            P.O. Box 217
            Station E
            Toronto, Ontario
            Canada, M6H 1H4

Dry Land Tourist

and other stories

DIANNE MAGUIRE

Sister Vision
Black Women and Women of Colour Press

Table of Contents

Dry Land Tourist

T he tall woman stood at the door for a long time. Her nose wrinkled as the odour of seasoning straw reached her. Ellen knew this place; her eyes wandered over it with familiarity. The sea breeze ruffled her blonde hair and pulled at her skirt, as if drawing her into the hall of the large Jamaican crafts market. Inside, the dark smiling market women waited for the sleepiness of the early afternoon to be dispelled by the next wave of tourists looking for gaudy beach hats, carved salad bowls and straw mats.

Ellen moved down the aisle, pausing to pick up a carving here, a basket there, nodding silently at the sales pitch of each vendor, cautious not to show too much interest in any one item. The market women smiled knowingly at each other as she passed beyond their stalls. They knew the type well; the tourist who must look at it all before parting with a few measly dollars.

And they were right. She had to choose the few gifts carefully. They would have to be tasteful and lightweight, these souvenirs of Jamaica she would send back to her friends in Canada. Halfway around the outer aisle of stalls her attention was drawn to a set of linen mats heavily embroidered with red hibiscus flowers. Just beyond them, further down the table, almost hidden from her view by the red madras-plaid skirts of the dolls propped against the stall, was a carved head of darkly stained mahogany. It stared out at her, a sombre statement surrounded by the silly painted smiles on doll heads wrapped in traditional cotton scarves. The carving spoke to her of the way things used to be, of the Jamaica of her childhood. The incongruity of the dark faced dolls with their red cheeks emphasized a familiar strength that lay beneath the surface of the mahogany portrait.

She picked up the head and cradled it in her hands, running her fingers over the smooth surface, tracing the rounded features, the generous nose, the firm chin of the handsome negro face. She tipped it upside down, looking for a signature.

"Someting wrong, missis?" If the vendor had spoken before, Ellen had not heard her.

"No, I'm looking for the artist's name."

"See't yah." The vendor's finger traced the zigzag marks in the wood at the base of the neck. "Is Ras Denzy mek dis one." The plump woman turned away, saying her next words as if to herself. "Him is a big-time artist uptown now... in him tam an all."

"Pardon?"

"Ras Denzy... He's one a dem Rastafari, wid di dreadlocks and di big tam. But high class people up town tink say him a big-time artist, so dem no mind di tam and di locks."

"Oh... How much is this?" Then began the usual haggling that is so much a part of market shopping. A price was finally agreed upon, and Ellen moved on to look at place mats and small bread baskets at another stall.

She was close enough to hear the market woman comment on her neighbour, "Yuh know, someting bout dat one mek me tink is a dry-land tourist dat."

"Ee-Hee, mi know wah yuh mean," was the other woman's reply.

Ellen looked over her shoulder at them. The market woman still had her newly acquired dollars in her hand. Her friend was twisting the end of her head tie to tuck it back into the maze of wound fabric on her head.

The big, white, dust-splashed statue of Queen Victoria watched over the pier and the crafts market, and towered over Ellen as she stepped back into the glaring afternoon sun and made her way to her car. Even this part of Kingston had changed while she had been away at college. But at least these landmarks were still here. At least something remained to trigger memories of her childhood, and her teen years.

But they were not enough; not enough to counteract the hurt she felt at being called a 'dry-land tourist', that derogatory term for a Jamaican who plays at being a foreigner.

For a moment she sat in the too-warm car, looking through the bag of her new purchases on the seat beside her. She picked out the carving and looked at the signature again.

"You done good, Ras Denzy," she thought. "I wonder - if he would remember me, it we had met again, 'uptown'?"

Probably not. She had been just a girl with long legs that dangled from her scruffy shorts to rubber flip-flop sandals then. Ras Denzy had often come to the kitchen door to sell her mother fresh fish and shrimp from a box built behind the seat of his bicycle. Ellen had sat on the kitchen steps and listened to her mother and the Rastafarian talk over the news of the day before discussing the price of the shrimp that filled the pint-sized juice can used as a measure. Then Ras Denzy would ride away down the street, slowly enough for Ellen to run along behind, yet fast enough to keep her from catching up. It was their game. And when he got to the end of the block, he would wave, "Okay, Longalala! I gone!" and turn the corner, leaving her for his next customer. Ellen tucked the carving back into the bag. She would keep this memento for herself, with the hope that it would remind her of her childhood, of the subtleties that add up to 'home' that she had taken for granted in those days. It wasn't until this trip that she missed them.

Ellen had returned to Jamaica with her college friend, Cathy. They had thought themselves lucky to get teaching jobs in Kingston. The pay was poor, but it meant that she could get reacquainted with old friends there. She and Cathy moved into studio apartments in a block on Hope Road. Her Jamaican friends had told her how the crime rate had escalated over the years, so she was glad to have someone nearby.

Although in some ways her social life was almost like it had been before she had gone to study in Vancouver, now, at the parties, there were more expatriates than Jamaicans. Ellen felt comfortable with this motley crowd of teachers, accountants, and other professionals on short contracts. They seemed to think of her as one of them; even when they talked of home as being Toronto or Manchester. But she had never thought of her mother's little apartment in Victoria, British

Columbia, as home.

One afternoon, Ellen took a drive out to the house, to the place in Jamaica she had thought of as home during all those years away in Vancouver. The building was still there, hidden behind overgrown hibiscus bushes and uncut grass. The driveway had deep potholes, and goats wandered in past the cattle trap as if it wasn't there. There was a life of sorts going on around the empty house and she felt like an intruder.

On the back porch, she found the old wooden mortar and pestle her grandmother had used to make cornmeal. She picked up the long smooth pole and pounded it into the knee-high mortar in imitation of the movement she had watched as a child. The crudely-carved pieces had rolled around in her car trunk all the way back to Kingston.

The burglary happened a few weeks later. Ellen had come home late that afternoon from school. Still in her old work clothes, she felt hot and sticky and in need of a shower. As she got out of the car, Cathy came out to greet her.

"Have you got someone staying with you or something?" Cathy asked in a loud whisper.

"No. Why?"

"Because there's someone in your apartment. I heard them and I think I even saw them moving in there." She pointed up at Ellen's window.

"Oh damn, it must be a thief. Have you called the police yet?"

"No, I was waiting for you to come home, to be sure."

"Then call them now." Ellen started up the stairs to her door, then hesitated. She turned back to the old wooden mortar and pestle that stood at the foot of the stairs where she had left them, propped up among the plants. She tested the weight of the smooth pestle in her hands, then started up the stairs again.

She was only halfway up the stairs when the door of her apartment was flung open by a thin Rasta man with a shopping bag in his hand. He came quickly down the stairs, watching his own feet. Then he looked up and saw her and stopped.

"Is wah yuh a go do wid dat?" He pointed at the pestle in her hands. Then he looked around, alarmed to find his only escape route blocked by the tenants gathered at the stairwell.

"Maybe hit you, hard. Those are my things you have," she replied, poking the pestle at the bag he held. He dropped the bag, and only hesitated to grimace at her before running back up the stairs and slamming the apartment door behind him.

Ellen could hear him pushing things around in the room. "Maybe he's looking for a weapon," she thought. It was only then that she realised how foolhardy she had been. She backed slowly down the steps and thunked the pestle back into the old mortar. Cathy was waiting for her.

"I've called the police. They're on their way."

"I wish I could stop him from doing any more damage in there."

"No. Don't be silly. He'd attack you!"

The siren's wail called out all the neighbours. Soon, the parking area was full of people and the policemen were pushing through them. They wouldn't let Ellen go with them. "Missis, yuh don't need to see this kind a violence." The policeman pronounced the last word as if it were exotic and foreign. But it wasn't. It was real and frightening. They could all hear the shouts and cries from where they stood waiting in the parking lot.

"Come out a deh! Come out a di cupboard!" The thief

had apparently hidden behind suitcases in the cupboard over the wardrobe. The sound of falling suitcases muffled his fall. But the sounds of punches to his thin body were punctuated by his cries for mercy.

Ellen thought one of two blows might be needed to subdue the struggling man. But ten minutes later, the cries were even louder and the beating hadn't stopped. She didn't want him killed, just her things back. She started towards the stairs, but Cathy grabbed her arm.

"No! Don't go in there."

"I've got to stop them. It's enough!"

"But you can't go up there now." Cathy's grip got tighter.

"But they have beaten him enough." Then Ellen screamed "Stop! STOP!"

A policeman appeared at the top of the stairs. "What's wrong?" he called.

"Stop the beating! Stop it!" Ellen shouted.

The policeman turned away and called into the apartment. "Better tek him out a yah. Di lady a distress herself."

Ellen watched the skinny Rasta stumble down the stairs, his hands held firmly behind him. He was sniffling and twisting about, trying to wipe blood from his forehead.

"Why yuh nuh run, bwoy? Eeh?" The policeman behind him pushed him towards the police car. "Run nuh, man. Run, mek me shoot yuh." The policemen laughed.

They shoved him into the back of the car. One man raised his heavy-booted foot and kicked the young man as he slumped on the seat. There was a long, loud wail from the back of the car.

Ellen stood watching it all, stunned, shaking her head in disbelief, as the senior officer came up to her.

"We'll take care of dis one fi yuh, ma'am."

"Will you need my things, the ones in the bag, for evidence?"

"Oh no, ma'am. Dere's no room in di prison fi small fry like dis one. But we gwine teach im a lesson all di same." He laughed as he joined his colleagues in the car.

Ellen was returning from another late afternoon spent on the school production scenery. She had slung her canvas bag on to her shoulder and was locking her car when she noticed Cathy's door was ajar. They had all been extra cautious about leaving doors open and unwatched since the robbery, so Ellen assumed that Cathy was just inside trying to cope with the summer heat.

She went up to knock on the door. Then she saw all the boxes and Cathy folding something into a suitcase. Cathy looked up and said, "I'm going back home."

"Just like that?"

"No, that business with the thief was just the last straw. And too close for comfort."

Cathy left within the week. Ellen had taken her out to the airport. She had felt numb as she waved back at the familiar face. For Cathy, Vancouver was home, and although she was sad to see her friend leave, Ellen knew it was best. But what was best for her, for Ellen? After all, this was supposed to be home.

She had been home from the airport for only about an hour when Ellen heard a knock on her door. She hadn't expected anyone, in fact, she thought most people in the building were still at the beach on that warm Sunday afternoon. She slipped the chain guard into place and opened the door just wide enough to see a man's face in the gloom of the hallway. The face was cut and bruised, yet vaguely familiar. Then she realized that it must be the thief, the man who had tried to rob her only a few days before. She started to close the door as she asked, "What do you want?"

"Miss Ellen?"

She opened the door again, and peered past the chain to take another look at the face on the other side. The man was not as young as she had thought he was on the night of the robbery. And the creases about his mouth and eyes had a familiarity about them that went beyond the fleeting glimpses she had had of a frightened face. She knew this man.

"Miss Ellen. Is Ras Denzy."

She could not answer him, her throat was too tight. Besides, what could she say?"

"Oh gawd, chile, I sorry!" He started to push at the door. "Truly, I sorry. I didn't know it was yuh."

"But why, Ras Denzy? When you're doing so well?"

"Yuh mean di art ting? Di money not steady." He came closer and pushed a shaking hand, palm up through the door at her. "Times hard, Miss Ellen. I beg yuh a little someting."

Ellen looked at the calloused hand. With him pressed against the door, she could smell the sweet scent of ganja that clung to his clothes. "No. I mean, wait." She reached for her purse and pulled out a five dollar bill.

The hand slowly retreated from sight. Then she heard Ras Denzy suck his teeth and mumble, "Dis no nuff fi notten at all." Ellen pushed the door shut and turned the deadbolt lock.

"I would never trouble yuh, chile," he called through the door. And when she didn't answer, "I sorry, yuh hear."

After a moment, that seemed longer to Ellen, slow footfalls echoed down the stairwell. She let out the breath she was holding and turned away from the door.

As she stepped back into the room, her eyes fell on the carved head on the bookcase. Its stare was hard and uncompromising.

Ellen picked up the carving and went into the kitchen. She wrapped it in paper towels. Then she pulled a cardboard box from under the table and returned to the bookcase. She wedged the carving into the corner of the box and started to fill the box with the items on the bookcase shelves.

Love Powder

I knew from the first time I set eyes on Joshua that something was going to happen. Not something bad, mind you, just a ruckus or the like.

He was standing at the gate talking to Mass Johnny, and even from the fowl-house I could see he was a dandy man, his pants legs creased so fine, and his pretty shirt collar turned back just so. And his fool head was nodding up and down like one of them plastic dogs boasy people put in their car windows.

Why Mass Johnny did tek him on I'll never understand, 'cause he looked too mawga and sickly to do a good day's work. In his heavy khaki work things his arms and legs looked small and lost and too weak to work a hillside farm like Mass Johnny's. And his skin always looked kind of grey and pasty brown. Perhaps that's why Mass Johnny agreed to put up with him. He was Teacher MacLaren's outside child.

So the next day Joshua came to work to tend the yam hills and clean the banana patch, pick coffee and dig ginger root. And I had to work with him, because that was why Mass Johnny let me stay in the yard with my Aunt Mattie. When I was done with school for the day, I had to help with the farm work, feeding fowl and hogs, collecting eggs and peeling ginger.

Peeling ginger is a tricky business. I never like doing it because of the hot juice. And it was that juice that cause me to look for a chance to get back at Joshua.

One day after school he called me as I started down the hill from the gate. "Vernon, don't drag yuh foot up deh, bwoy." He flapped his long fingered hand at me. "I want these gingers on the barbecue tonight, so start to peel."

I put down my books on the edge of the concrete barbecue and sat beside my Aunt Mattie. As I took a knife and a ginger root from her I asked, "What a bodder him today?"

"Mass Johnny all but call him lazy, so him have to take it out on yuh and me. Yuh know how it go, kick dog bite cat."

Now I'm no expert when it comes to peeling ginger root, but I follow what I see my Aunt Mattie and the other women doing. I cut up and down between the fingers of the root first, and then slice away the flat part. I was just holding a root firm to pull the blade across the skin to cut it away when Joshua came up to me and said "See that yuh do it right, bwoy." And as he passed he hit me on the shoulder, the one that was attached to the hand with the knife. The blade jerked into the ginger and I gripped hard with my other hand, the one holding the root, so I wouldn't drop it. But I squeezed it and the juice jumped right out of that root and into my eye.

Well, as you can imagine, I dropped the root and the knife and let out one holler, "Me eye! Me eye! It a bun me eye!" The juice in my eye burned so that I jumped up and knocked the books into the dirt.

Aunt Mattie pulled me to the catchment tank and turned on the tap to full. She splashed my face with the water. "Come, chile, wash it out here. Open di eye and wash it out." She pulled my head right under the tap and the water splashed all over the front of my clothes. It wet through everything, to the skin, and still my eye hurt me.

"Dat damn fool Joshua, he don't know not to fool round someone wid ginger and a knife." Auntie Mattie tugged at the buttons of my shirt. "How's di eye now?"

"It still hurt, but is better." I was crying but there was so much water on my face, she couldn't see it.

"Let me see." She looked into the eye, pulling the bottom lid down.

"Oh Miss Mattie, im alright?" Joshua had come over to see what was going on. He put a hand on Aunt Mattie's shoulder, and the bushy curls of his eyebrows almost met high on his forehead he was frowning so hard. But it was the hurt on his face when Aunt Mattie looked at his hand with scorn and shook her shoulder to tell him to take it off that told me to watch him with my auntie.

Aunt Mattie was bound and determined to get my shirt off me. And when she saw that all my clothes were wet, she wanted me to take everything off. Well, that was alright. My short pants were getting cold against my legs and sticking to my skin. But when she wanted my briefs, I stopped. I'm too old to run about the yard with everything out there for people to see.

I could hear the women at the barbecue laughing at me and I turned to see two of Mass Johnnie's little yellow-head daughters snickering behind their hands.

"Come bwoy, don't be stupid." Auntie Mattie tugged at my briefs. "Give me dese so I can hang dem to dry."

And she pulled them down, almost to my knees. The girls shrieked with laughter. I started to run across the yard, but the briefs slipped lower and tighter around my knees. I felt I would fall so I stopped and took di stupid briefs off and ran into Aunt Mattie's room.

It took days for me to live down that shame. Every time Mass Johnnie's daughters looked at me in the yard, they would giggle together and whisper something about my 'little brown batty'. But one of them was my friend; Miss Bea with the curly yellow hair and long white legs. She spoke to me nice and friendly right from the first time I moved into Aunt Mattie's room and didn't snub me at school like her sister, Esmie. And she started to tell the others to leave me alone and stop the teasing.

Only Joshua wouldn't leave me alone. He started to take me with him out to the yam hills and the coffee piece. Each afternoon he would come to the pantry and call out "Miss Mattie, could I trouble yuh for a little ice water?"

"Yes, yes, alright." And Aunt Mattie would pour him a cup of ice water and pass it to him with such impatience half the water would slop out of the cup.

"Thank yuh, Miss Mattie." Joshua would drink slowly, all the while eyeing my plump and comely auntie from where he stood by the pantry door. He would work his mouth as if he had something else to say. Then he would look for me and call, "Come on, bwoy. Time for me and yuh to do a little work." And he would hustle me away to the banana patch, the pig sty, in whichever direction he was facing when he saw me. There wasn't always work there, but I was usually the only one there to see his pasty light-skin face blush.

At first he only talked about work, pigs and coffee

beans and the like. But one afternoon he blushed so much that I couldn't stop from laughing. He caught me snickering into my hand and blushed even more. "It's cause I'm shy, bwoy, just shy," he mumbled and turned to do something else.

But I knew better, and I knew that I only had to wait and watch to get a chance to get back at Joshua for the business with the ginger. After all, it was my auntie he was blushing over.

Joshua remembered that soon enough and started to say things like, "She's a fine lady, yuh Aunt Mattie; a fine lady," to me each time we went out to do the afternoon work. Then he got up the courage to ask me if I thought she liked him. I did think it was wise to say, "She like everybody in her fashion."

And it is the truth I did speak. She didn't carry grudges like so many women like her - oldish and without a man, and cooking for somebody else's family. But you knew she wouldn't stand for any nonsense when she stood over you with her big hands on her wide hips. But as I said to my friend Bea when I told her about Joshua being in love with my Aunt Mattie, I couldn't see her really liking a skinny dandyman like Joshua. She was too big and brown and pretty for him.

It was Bea who gave me the idea when she said, "It would take some serious obeah to get Mattie to fall for that ugly, mawga man."

The very next afternoon, when Joshua dragged me off to the banana patch to clear trash, I waited for him to make his usual comment about Aunt Mattie. I suggested, "Perhaps the Obeah-man have someting to help yuh."

"What yuh mean - 'help' me?" asked Joshua.

"I see yuh face a red-up every time yuh talk to mi Aunt Mattie. So I thought - maybe the Obeah-man know how to help yuh in dat department."

"The Obeah-man, eh?... Humph." He walked into the next row of trees and worked without a word for the rest of the afternoon.

That Saturday Joshua dressed in his fancy trousers, the ones with the fine, fine creases, and he walked into town. But when Bea and I went to buy some jujubes and snowcones with our pocket money, we didn't see Joshua any place at all. He came back late in the day with a funny look on his face as if he'd done something very smart.

Sunday after church, I found out what gave him that look. He stopped me at the gate and pulled me by the arm to one side of the catchment tank. "I need yuh to do something for me," he said.

"But is Sunday, sah!"

"Please do dis fi me - and don't tell anybody mi send yuh."

"Send me where, sah?" I got curious.

"To di Pharmacy. I have a paper here wid di scription on it. Tek it and dese two dollar and bring it to me when yuh see me alone."

"Alright," I said. "But let me tek off me church clothes first." And I took the money and the paper into Aunt Mattie's room.

She was in there putting on a clean apron and cap, like she always did for Sunday dinner. I put the money and paper on the bureau and started to change my clothes.

"Is what dat?" she asked, picking up the paper.

"Someting Joshua ask me to get fi him."

She unfold the paper and read it, "Two ounces Love Powder?"

"I tell yuh, is someting Joshua ask me to pick up at

di Pharmacy. See di money fi it yah so." I picked up the
two dollars and tucked them into my short's pocket.

"Love Powder - fi who?"

I tried to keep my face straight. "Fi yuh. Is yuh him
in love wid."

I'd never heard my Aunt Mattie laugh so hard. She
hugged herself about her big chest and rocked back,
laughing until she hit the bed. "Me! Ha! Ha! Di poor
bwoy!" She was almost crying she was laughing so hard.

I let out my laugh too. "So yuh don't want dis mawga
man to love yuh?"

"No, no!" And her laugh grew louder again.

"So what me going do wid di money?"

"Go buy bulla-cake fi supper."

"Bulla? Oh yes!" And I left for town and old Miss
Clarice little corner shop that open all hours and sell the
best bulla-cake in town.

It wasn't until the next afternoon that Joshua
caught me on my own to ask about his powder. "Did yuh
get it? Yuh have it to give me?"

"Not now. Me don't carry it around wid me," I said.
"Not safe, man."

"Yes, of course. But yuh can get it fi mi now?"

"You'll wait for me here?"

"Yes, yes. But go fetch it now."

I left him digging hills and humming to himself. I
ran back to the pantry and almost tripped on the steps
up to the door. "Aunt Mattie! He want the powder now!"
I blurted out before I saw that she was not alone. Bea
and Esmie were standing there, at Auntie's elbow,
waiting to lick the bowl she was mixing cake icing in.

Of course, they wanted to know what it was all
about. I looked at Aunt Mattie to see what she thought
we should tell them. She shrugged and said, "Cho, di

bwoy so fool yuh may as well tell dem 'bout it."

So I told them about the powder and the bulla-cakes and how Joshua now wanted his powder. "Wah mi a go do? Weh mi going to get powder to give him?"

Esmie was the first to have an idea. "Flour! It fine and sprinkle easy and mix well. It's perfect whatever he do wid it."

"Yes, but if him lick it off his finger, he'll know dat is flour," said Aunt Mattie. "And den is trouble fi yuh, bwoy!"

Bea stood nearest the window looking out just in case Joshua followed me. Suddenly she jumped up and down. "I know, I know what yuh can use!" She pointed out the window. "Lime, the lime powder Papa mixes to whitewash the kitchen wall."

Leaning against the stone section of the kitchen wall, next to a whitewash brush in a bucket, was a bag of lime. I was about to go out to look at the lime when Aunt Mattie stopped me. "Yuh need a paper to wrap it in."

"Yes, to wrap it like they do in di Pharmacy." said Esmie.

"Mama's writing paper, dat's what yuh need." Bea ran out of the pantry and soon returned with a sheet of white paper. We all went out to the lime. A little scoop was enough, and I folded the paper clean and smart like the pharmacist would.

Then I ran back to Joshua with it. He just put it into his breast pocket without a word about what he was going to do with it.

I was too curious to leave it at that, so I watched him. He did nothing out of the ordinary all afternoon. But late that evening he came out of his room dressed in his fancy, sharp-creased pants. He walked across the yard to where Aunt Mattie sat under the guava tree.

She liked to spend the cool of the evening listening to the crickets sing. So she was sitting on an old kitchen chair by the tree when Joshua came over to her and asked if he could join her.

"Oh yuh bring a chair and I can't quarrel wid where yuh sit," she answered him.

He went into the kitchen and brought out a chair, but he stopped at the door and put it down. Then he took a big white kerchief and spread it on the seat of the chair. He took the paper-wrapped powder from his breast pocket and emptied it into the handkerchief. Then he folded the kerchief and tucked it into his pants pocket, and picked up the chair and went over to put it down next to Aunt Mattie.

Bea, Esmie and I were in the pantry, drinking orange juice, when we heard Joshua first speak to Aunt Mattie. We gathered at the window to watch and listen. Bea whispered into my ear. "Yuh tink him going use the powder now?"

"But what him going do wid it?" asked Esmie, a little too loudly. Afraid he might hear, Bea and I shushed her and ducked down below the counter. A moment later we heard him speak again and sneaked a look. But he didn't say anything, just "Ah hum." He cleared his throat and squirmed on his chair as if something was biting him in his pants. At last he said, "Di crickets singing real sweet dis evening, eh, Miss Mattie?"

"Yes, Mr. Joshua," replied Aunt Mattie, without turning to look at him.

"I would say," he cleared his throat again, "that your voice would sound as sweet if yuh was to sing."

"Well, I don't sing."

Joshua sighed and his bony shoulders sank over his hollow chest. He looked down at his feet for a while before he looked for the kerchief sticking out of his pocket. As he pulled it out, he straightened his shoulders. He cleared his throat and said, "My, is a warm evening, eh, Miss Mattie?" And with a flourish he flicked his kerchief open, sprinkling fine white powder all over Aunt Mattie.

She sat looking at him for a moment, with her mouth open in astonishment. Then she laughed and laughed and jumped up to shake off the powder. The girls and I couldn't hold back any longer and ran out to laugh with Aunt Mattie.

Joshua looked confused for a minute and when he realized what had been going on, he turned away, his face all screwed up and red.

Then Aunt Mattie cried out, "Lawd-a-mercy! Look what yuh do, chile!"

Bea had carried her orange juice with her out to the yard and, in the excitement, she spilt some on to Aunt Mattie, on to her arm where the lime powder was sprinkled.

"Rahtid! It a bun me!" Aunt Mattie squeezed her arm and started to run to the catchment tank. But Joshua was there before her. He wet his kerchief and filled the old chipped enamel pan that was always there by the tap, and brought them to Aunt Mattie.

"Here." He wiped her arm with his kerchief. "Hold yuh hand out so I won't wet yuh." And he splashed a little water from the pan on to her arm.

"Ah, dat's better," said Aunt Mattie. "Thank yuh," and she looked at Joshua and smiled. And what is worse, he smile on her, too.

The Funeral

"Bea! Bee..ea!"

Bea peered through the wooden slate of latticework at Mattie, the cook, who was striding across the yard, calling at the top of her voice, "Bea! Bee...ea!

Mattie stopped at the bottom of the back steps. She bent forward as she retied her apron. "Weh di rass is dat child? As if there's not enough to do wid dis funeral. Bea! Come put on yuh church dress!"

Bea watched Mattie climb the steps into the pantry, the cook's new shoes squeaking with each step. She'd been holding her breath. As Mattie disappeared behind the screen door, Bea took in a deep breath and then stifled a sneeze. For a moment she had forgotten how close she was to the dust covered latticework that concealed her hiding place under the house.

She had climbed under the back steps to hide under the house as soon as her mother had said it was time to get ready for the funeral. She didn't want to go to the funeral. She hadn't really known Grandpa anyway.

Besides she couldn't even remember what he looked like.

Dead things made Bea feel queasy. She didn't even like watching Mattie clean a chicken. And she had a nightmare the last time the cat brought a dead mouse into the house. So seeing a dead person would be too much. She would faint or be sick for sure. It was better to have her mother angry at her for disappearing before the funeral instead. At least this time she would be out of the way.

How angry could her mother get? After all, Bea had spent the morning helping to get the house ready; making the beds and dusting the parlour. She had even helped her sister Esmie spread the table with the damask cloth and the fancy china.

That was the only chore Esmie actually did that morning. She always managed to get other people to do her jobs for her. Their mother, Emma, never seemed to notice, or maybe she didn't care. Bea hated it when her mother shouted at them all, "I can't do everything around here!" After all, the chores got done anyway. And it was usually Bea who did them.

Bea could hear her mother's voice, loud and strong, calling her from inside the house. "Bea, where are you, child?" She heard the screen door bang and her mother's slippers slap down the steps. "I don't have time for yuh nonsense. Bea! Dem chickens making noise so the fowlhouse roof going come off. Bea! I want to see yuh dressed when I done with the chickens."

Bea stepped back from the latticework. She held her body tight, wrapped in her arms. She watched her mother cross the yard and enter the fowlhouse.

It was cool and dark under the house. Bea didn't like it there. The dust kept getting into her nose and making her sneeze or cough. It smelled frowzy and old. The ground sloped sharply up to the narrow space under the front verandah. It got very dark up there. And there was no way of knowing what was in that dark place. Or even in the dirt by the back steps; Bea knew a praying mantis had been killed there only last week. And her brother Darrell had claimed a scorpion used to live there.

This place was Darrell's. He hid under the house every Sunday. It wasn't really hiding anymore. Everyone knew that was where he went to get out of going to church. It didn't work either. He'd come out when his father told him about the beating he'd give him when he got back from the service.

The noise from the fowl-house got louder again. Bea looked through the latticework at her mother shuffling her way back to the pantry, a basket of eggs in her hand. "Mattie!" Emma called out. "Is what dat I smell burning?"

"De biscuits, Ma'am." Mattie shouted from the kitchen door. "I just taking dem out di oven."

"And yuh let dem burn!"

"No, Ma'am. Dem alright."

But Emma had to go see for herself. Bea backed up the slope away from the steps. She was afraid that the more her mother walked up and down, the more she was likely to find her hiding place. She hit her head against a beam and swallowed the dryness in her throat. She rubbed the spot and winced at the cobwebs she found there. Bea shivered at the thought of spiders crawling over her. She ran her hands over her shoulders and through her hair.

She hated her hair; so yellow and curly like her Papa's. It had caused her much unhappiness. It began with Darrell pulling at it. Her mother would plait Bea's hair in the morning and by midday Darrell would have worried and pulled and teased until the plaits were half undone. Bea would cry and try to fight him off, but she was too small then.

Darrell went off to boarding school and Bea went to the local elementary. The boys there pulled her plaits too, so her mother tied them together on top of her head with a ribbon. But at playtime the other children would reach out and touch her hair and her face. It was as if she was the only one with fair skin and yellow hair. Esmie would slap their hands hard, but Bea couldn't do that. She always thought of how it would hurt her hand too. And she was too shy to try to touch her classmate's tight curls and brown skin. But she wondered what it would feel like.

Her plaits came loose as Bea searched for spiders and cobwebs. Her mother went back into the pantry and Bea moved back to the latticework to look out at the yard again. The dog was half-heartedly chasing a chicken in the midday sun. She wondered if her mother was still looking for her. Then she heard the clomp of her father's work boots overhead and her mother's shout, "Tek off dem dirty boots before yuh walk in a dis house, Johnny."

"Cho, mi too tired fi stop out a door!" Papa shouted back. His cough was almost as loud as the scrape of his boots on the wooden floor, and it went on long after his footfalls stopped.

"What I tell yuh bout yuh cough, Johnny?" Emma called back. "Yuh going dead before yuh reach doctor!"

Papa started to cough again, and gasped out a reply that Bea couldn't hear. She could only hear the coughing go on. She wondered if one day Papa wouldn't be able to stop, and he wouldn't get his breath and would die like her mother said.

Lighter footsteps sounded overhead and the screen door slammed to a shout of "Come back here, bwoy!" Darrell leapt down the steps and rolled under them into the gap in the latticework.

"What di rass yuh doing here?" he asked as soon as he saw Bea.

She stepped aside to let him in. "Mi nah go to no funeral. Mi don't want to see dead smaddy."

"Nor hear di preacher go on 'bout what a good man Grandpa was."

"I didn't know him. So why I must be dere when him dead and bury?"

"Is not me yuh haffi convince!" said Darrell, brushing the dust from his short pants. "But dis a fi me place. So yuh mus come out now."

"Can't I stay? Just until dem gone to the funeral?"

"No, I don't like nobody in here."

"Just dis one time, please?"

"No! Come out!" Darrell pushed her towards the gap in the latticework.

"Shush! Dem will find us!" Bea held on to the lattice, her fingers poking through the gaps in the wooden slats.

"Den if yuh come out dem won't find me here."

"Maybe dem will see me leaving." Bea wiped her hands, trying to rid them of dust.

Darrell didn't have a chance to answer. Mattie and Emma came clattering down the steps. "Now we know where Darrell is... so mek we get dem pickney ready fi di service. Darrell! Darree..ell!"

Bea and Darrell looked at each other. From the sound of her voice, they knew their mother meant business.

"Boy, I know yuh in there!" she shouted. "So yuh come out and bring Bea wid yuh!"

Darrell pushed Bea, catching her off balance. She fell forward on to the ground under the steps. "No!" she cried, and tears began to fill her eyes. Mattie pulled at her, urging her to her feet. She twisted about and resisted the firm grip Mattie had on her as she was pushed up the steps into the house.

Bea was scrubbed and tidied. Her plaits were redone and tied with white ribbons. Her pale blue church dress looked plain without its satin sash.

Mattie watched Bea and Darrell until their mother was ready to leave for the funeral. She made them sit on chairs in the pantry and watch her as she cut sandwiches into little triangles. They were for after the service, when everyone would come back to the house. Esmie danced in and out of the room, calling them, "Rude chile". Bea didn't pay her any mind. She looked out the window and watched the dog circle and settle, and snap at flies.

Bea and Darrell sat quite still when their mother, dressed in a black frock and hat, held them up by the ear and told them what would happen if they misbehaved. She kept them close to her all the way to the funeral. As they stepped into the church, Bea saw the open coffin up near the altar. She began to whimper and couldn't stop when her mother hit her shoulder with a "Shush". Then she pulled Bea forward.

"I don't want to go up dere," wailed Bea, turning away from her mother's hand.

"Mi no tell yuh to behave?" hissed her mother.

"But mi nuh want to see nobody dead!" Bea cried.

Darrell bent over and said in a loud whisper, "Yuh may as well be quiet now yuh is here." Then he helped his mother push Bea forward.

"Mi don't want to go up dere!" she whined. Everybody was looking at her. Emma and Darrell took her by the hand and pulled her, crying and jerking around, to the side of the coffin.

"Quiet, child. And pay yuh respects to yuh Grandpa.

See, yuh Grandpa dead." Her mother lifted her to look in at the body lying in the coffin.

Bea closed her eyes, squeezing out tears that ran down her cheeks and on to the collar of her dress. Then she stole a peek at the man in the coffin. That one glimpse so frightened her that her eyes popped wide open. She stopped sniffling and stared at the face - a face that was familiar.

Suddenly she screamed, "No, dat's Papa. Him hair white but is mi Papa. Mi Papa's no dead! What him doing dere?" She turned around and back and escaped her mother's grip.

"Shush!" said Emma, reaching out to stroke Bea's head. "Is not yuh Papa. Is Grandpa."

"No, is Papa... wid white hair. My Papa!" Bea screamed again and ran from the church.

She stumbled and tripped, the tears in her eyes blinding her as she rushed down the hill to the farm. She slipped at the gate and fell on to the grass. She cried out loud and beat the grassy slope with her fists until she ran out of breath and had to stop for air.

It was her Papa. It looked like him, but why did he have white hair? And why was he so thin, his face all wrinkled? Bea pulled up her socks and brushed the grass on her skirt. She rubbed at tears with the back of her hand and walked slowly toward the house. She stopped by the front verandah for a moment, then ran around to the back steps and pulled her skirt about her as she ducked through the gap in the latticework.

She sat on the ground and hugged her knees. She sat there and watched the dog come into the yard and lie down near the fowlhouse. Mattie came out of the kitchen, carrying a plate of biscuits into the pantry. The service would be over soon enough. She would wait here and see if her Papa came back.

The Sanitary Inspector

"Ah who dat goin out di gate, Mattie?"

"Joe 'Neezer, ma'am."

I watched the little black man, too. He walked up to the gate with his back straight and his head high, like he's somebody, even though he now limped. I smiled to see him dragging that foot, big with a dirty bandage and strapped into an old sandal. Everybody called him 'Neezer but not to his face. To him, you always say "Mr. Johnstone." But I wonder if he did know he was named from that Christmas story about the ghost and one Scrooge.

"What him have to say?" Miss Emma called back.

"Notten new," answered my Aunt Mattie. "But yuh know how him love to chat, Ma'am!"

"Uh huh," Miss Emma laughs like her chickens. Cackle, cackle, cackle. "I hope yuh not tellin him how tings stay here."

"No, ma'am. But him try more ways fi ask."

"Dat man gossip like an old woman," cackled Miss Emma.

"Yes. But him only tell it when it suit him."

"Uh huh, uh huh," Miss Emma nodded. "When him done use it."

There was another time that I heard Miss Emma and my Aunt Mattie, talking about 'Neezer. I heard them because they were baking bread in the kitchen and I was outside whitewashing the stone wall.

Aunt Mattie had said, "Ma'am, Joe 'Neezer was here dis morning... inspecting di pit latrine and how much Jeyes disinfectant down dere."

"He must love di work, him come here so often."

"Yes, ma'am. Him look all into di pit at di Jeyes and di flies." And I saw her put a finger under her nose as she copied how 'Neezer turned his mustache about his face and say "Nuff Jeyes here, not much flies."

Miss Emma laughed, "Uh huh, he poke his nose into everybody's business."

"It seems like him mind Mass Williams' business to his advantage."

"How dat?"

"Well, ma'am, he did buy out Mass Williams' land and sell it to some man from Mandeville fi plenty money."

"He's up to dat again?" said Miss Emma. "He did dat with Obie Brown's place, yuh know. Miss Myrtle fool enough to tell him how hard times tek dem one day when him stop to inspect di pit toilet and he went right out to Obie in di coffee piece and mek him an offer, just so."

"An Mass Obie tek di offer?"

"He thought it was di best he would get. But 'Neezer, he went over to Christiana and found some young man just back from foreign wid money burning a hole in him pocket. And he carry him and buy di property fi half as much again."

I finished painting the wall and had to go wash out

the brush. But I remembered that talk when Joshua, my Aunt Mattie's boyfriend, asked me a little advice. He and I come to be friends some years ago with the business of the love powder that I was to fetch for him to help my Aunt Mattie look on him with love in her eye. It was I who sent him to the Obeah-man, and the love powder did work somehow.

One afternoon when I was helping Joshua with Mass Johnny's yam hills, he started to tell me about how he would never do well as long as he stayed here working for Mass Johnny and Miss Emma. That Aunt Mattie would never take him seriously, poor as he was. That he must go abroad to make some serious money. Then Aunt Mattie would marry him.

I thought he was just talking, but he talked about it almost every time we were out working together. It got so I started asking him why he didn't "just ups and go." At first he would tell me he hadn't decided which was the best place to go to; whether he could make enough in Kingston, or if it would be better to spend a few months in America with the farmworker program. But he really seemed to like the idea of going to Canada. He'd heard how people could get good jobs up there.

Then one day when I asked him why he didn't go, he answered me with a bark like a dog tired of chasing his fleas. "Yuh know I don't have di money fi di fare."

"Then why yuh don't borrow it?" I asked.

"Who yuh know have money like dat to lend?" he grumbled.

That's when I remembered what I'd heard, "Joe 'Neezer."

At first Joshua didn't believe me. After all, Joe 'Neezer didn't have a car or a house. He lived in rooms over Harry MacCauley's shop and would only ride his bicycle when he had to go out to inspect pit latrines far out in the country.

But the next day Joshua brought it up again.

"So, Vernon, yuh sure Joe 'Neezer have di money. Yuh tink him would lend me di fare to Canada?"

"Yes, man."

"Uh hum," and then he didn't say anything.

"No, I going to think bout it."

He didn't think about it for long. That Saturday Joshua came to my Aunt Mattie's room at Mass Johnny's and called me outside and asked, "Yuh coming wid me to look for Joe 'Neezer?"

"What I want wid Joe 'Neezer?" I asked.

"To borrow me fare to Canada."

"But is yuh want di money."

"Come wid me, man. Yuh can speak fi me."

So I went with him into town to see 'Neezer. We walked slowly up to the crossroads. Joshua kept saying something about not "hastening to debt." Harry MacCauley's shop on the corner was a dark, dusty place full of dry goods. Buckets and brooms out by the door almost tripped us up as we walked around looking for the stairs up to the rooms where Joe 'Neezer lived.

We found them at the back of the shop, old and rickety, with peeling paint. Joshua took his time going up the stairs but he slipped when he set foot on a broken step a third of the way up the stairs. He would have fallen to the ground if I hadn't caught him.

"Lawd, what if is duppy push me!" he cried. "What if it is a signal that I mustn't ask fi dis money, Vernon?"

"Look, man, is piece gone from di step." I pointed at the broken stair. "Is alright. Go on up." And I pushed him back up the stairs.

"Yes, yes," and he pulled his shirt straight and climbed the steps to the back verandah. There were three doors there and he stood a long while trying to decide which one to knock on. He finally knocked on the middle door, and then stepped back to the railing as if afraid of what he would see when the door opened.

A young woman opened the door. She had bright even teeth in her smile and her light brown skin was so smooth and pretty I wanted to reach out and touch it.

"Yes, sah?" she asked.

"Ah looking fi Mass Nz... Johnstone," Joshua stammered.

"He's not here, sah."

"Not here? Den where can I find him?"

"Don't know, sah. Him always out a door, talking to dis one, calling to dat one." Her long arms gestured toward the street.

"But I need to talk wid him," whined Joshua.

"Den yuh have to go look fi him. Like me when dinner ready... up and down di street a call him like some old fisher'oman." She pouted and placed a hand on her hip.

"Which way him gone?" asked Joshua as he started to leave.

"Yuh no tink I woulda tell yuh if I did know?" She sucked her teeth noisily and closed the door. So we went back down to the street.

"Now where to start, dat's di ting." Joshua scratched his head.

"Maybe if yuh tek dat side and I go down so, we find him quicker," I suggested.

"No, den if I find him first, yuh won't be dere to speak fi mi."

I shrugged and went along with him.

"Come mek we check out di rum shop first," said Joshua. But we stopped in MacCauley's shop and he sent me up and down the narrow aisles of the shop, kicking up the dust 'til I started to sneeze. And then we stopped to ask old Henry, the tailor, if he had seen 'Neezer anywhere.

"Somebody did pass here, but I never look to see is who," he said.

When we reached the rum shop we could see that people were gathered in there. The radio was playing some calypso tune and the voices of the drinkers got louder as we went in the door. 'Neezer sat by the counter, tipping his chair back, his little moustache working about under his nose as he spoke: "And did yuh hear bout George Williams' daughter, how she..."

"Excuse, Mass Johnstone." Joshua interrupted him.

"Yuh no see I talking here, bwoy?"

"Sorry, sah." Joshua bobbed up and down. "Is serious business I come to talk wid yuh."

"Business, pon a Saturday?" 'Neezer sniffed, but he got up and came to the door.

"Please, sah, if I could speak wid yuh, out so." Joshua stepped aside to let him pass out of the shop.

"So what dis business bout?"

"Well, sah, it go like so. I tek it into mi mind to go to Canada, sah."

"Why yuh waan go Canada?"

"Dem have good jobs dere, sah. But I don't have di fare. I'm asking, sah, if yuh could see yuh way to lend me di money. When I reach Canada, I can work and send back di money fi yuh."

"An him is a good worker, sah. I work wid him, sah, an he's a good worker," I said, speaking for Joshua like I was suppose to do.

"What yuh here for, bwoy?" asked 'Neezer. "Dis is man to man talk. Yuh just run along."

"Me is here to speak fi him, sah," I protested.

"He can speak for himself." 'Neezer waved me away and I walked slowly down the street backwards, watching to see if I could tell from the way they moved their hands and talked whether or not Joshua would get his loan. But I couldn't. They nodded at each other and 'Neezer touched Joshua on the shoulder a couple of times. And then he shrugged and strolled back into the rum shop.

Joshua hurried down the street towards me. "Him say him going tink bout it... 'cause me no have nuff colatral, him call it. Me mus go see him four o'clock tomorrow."

Joshua got his loan and he left for Canada so fast, I didn't have time to think more of it. I don't know what Aunt Mattie thought of Joshua's going away because she never said anything about it. In fact, she was kind of quiet ever since the day he came to Mass Johnnie's place with the loan from Joe 'Neezer. She just said, "Well, I guess is alright."

But it wasn't alright. No sooner had Joshua sent to tell us about Canada than Joe 'Neezer came to inspect Mass Johnnie's pit latrine and to ask for Joshua's address. I could tell Aunt Mattie didn't want to give it to him; she played like she didn't know about the loan.

But nothing she did could help Joshua. It seems that it took him a little while to get a job and then when he did get work, it didn't pay as much as he thought it would. But he sent Mattie money for the loan and Joe 'Neezer came to collect. And everytime he would say, "Just interest, the boy only sent di interest." And he would walk up and down and poke at Aunt Mattie with his finger and talk about people "who bad and borrow money and won't pay anything but di interest"... until she would go into her own pocket money and find the extra money.

One day he came to collect the money from Aunt Mattie when Mass Johnnie's son, young Mass Darrell, and his cousin Horace were home from that big school in St. Elizabeth, the one I want to go to if I pass the Common Entrance Exam. The boys were getting ready to go shooting birds up on the Hill and Miss Emma was telling the boys to watch themselves with those guns when Aunt Mattie shouted, "I tell yuh, I don't have it!"

"Joshua must send yuh di money!" 'Neezer shook a finger at her face.

"I done give yuh what he did send me."

"I tell yuh it's not enough!" 'Neezer pushed Aunt Mattie's shoulder.

"Don't touch me!" Aunt Mattie screamed.

He pushed her again.

"Yuh don't hear me? Don't touch me!"

"Leave mi auntie alone!" I ran to her and stood between her and 'Neezer, ready to thump him.

'Neezer screwed up his face, like he smelled something stink. "Bwoy, draw wey, leave us. Is business we a talk," and he pushed me to one side.

"Yuh don't trouble mi auntie." I threatened him with my fists. I was ready to hit this nasty, ugly man, but Miss Emma came up behind me and caught my fist in her hand.

"No, Vernon, dat won't solve anything." Miss Emma pulled me away. "Go get a crocus bag fi di boys." And she pushed me towards the fowlhouse.

"Now what is dis about?" she asked.

When I came back with the crocus bag, I could see she was just as vexed with 'Neezer as I was.

"Yuh call dat interest!" she shouted. "Dat's daylight robbery!"

"Pardon, ma'am." 'Neezer's mustache twitched about as he closed his mouth hard and screwed up his face.

"Yuh heard me. It's wicked, charging dat kind a interest!" Miss Emma stood firm with her hands on her hips, a fierce scowl on her face.

"Is notten wrong wid charging interest when yuh lend money, ma'am." Joe 'Neezer pulled himself to his full height to look Miss Emma in the eye.

"It wrong to charge this much, and yuh know it." Miss Emma stepped toward 'Neezer who sniffed and walked away.

"I coming fi di rest tomorrow," he called to Aunt Mattie as he headed for the gate.

I started after him, "Yuh leave mi auntie alone!" But Miss Emma stopped me again.

"No, Vernon. yuh go wid di boys. Take di crocus bag and go wid di boys." She pulled me back and then Mass Darrell took a hold of my arm to lead me out towards the Hill.

I called out to Aunt Mattie, "Mi going wid dem. Is alright?"

Aunt Mattie put her hand to her head, like she was distressed. "Lawd, it hard, missis. It hard," she mumbled.

"I know, I know," Miss Emma gently touched Mattie's shoulder for a moment before she went back to the house.

So that morning, when Mass Darrell and his cousin Horace went up the hill to shoot birds, I went with them to carry the crocus bag to put the dead birds in. We walked around through those wild orange trees the birds love so. I went ahead sometimes, to scare the birds out of the bush. Mass Darrell shot two and then Horace got one; and by the time they decided that I should try my hand at shooting, we were all the way over by the Harrison place.

Darrell gave me the 12-bore gun and showed me how to hold it and how to look down the barrel at the target. I looked at the bushes and trees, then at the fence by the Harrison's place. There was a crow perched on the barbed wire. I looked down the barrel at it and noticed someone moving just beyond the crow. I moved the gun to follow him and squinted down the barrel at the sanitary inspector checking out the Harrison's outhouse... at the same Joe 'Neezer who was taking money from Aunt Mattie and Joshua.

I watched 'Neezer inspect the pit latrine, walk around it, bending and sniffing. I knew it was that wicked man, even though I couldn't really see his screwed up, ugly face. I still wanted to hit him, to stop him hurting my Aunt Mattie. After all, it was my fault that Joshua got the loan from him in the first place. When he closed the door of the outhouse, the crow on the fence took off and I pulled the trigger.

"What yuh want to shoot a crow for?' asked Darrell.

"Oh, I..." I felt foolish. "Mi never know it was a crow. Can't see for sure from here."

I didn't always see Joe 'Neezer when he came to collect the loan money. But whenever Aunt Mattie got a letter from Joshua she would sit quietly with a sad look on her face. When I asked her 'what wrong' she would just say, "Life hard, sah, life hard." And I knew that it was 'Neezer who made it so hard.

The day that he came to inspect the pit latrine at Mass Johnnie's again, it just happened that I had found an old machete at the back of the fowlhouse. There was a file there too, and I had sharpened the machete with the file like I used to see Joshua do. Then I went out to the banana patch beyond the coffee piece, and started to chop at the stumps of banana trees harvested in the past week. I was out there cutting into the core of a stump still green when I saw 'Neezer with Aunt Mattie, walking about the outhouse.

"Yuh know, is my design dis," he said to Aunt Mattie. "Is a government approve design too. Dat's why yuh don't have no trouble wid dis one. Is my good design." He strutted like he was so important. He opened the door and looked in, "Nuff Jeyes."

When he closed the door he sniffed and nodded at Aunt Mattie. Then he saw me. He stepped carefully through the banana patch as if to save his shoes from some fowl mess. "What yuh doing dere, boy?" he called.

"Notten, sah." I didn't want to talk to him.

"What yuh mean notten. What yuh have doing wid dat machete?"

"Chopping banana stump, sah."

"Dat's foolishness. Mind yuh don't cut yuhself."

"Sah." I went on chopping at the stumps. He stepped closer and reached out as if to stop me. I stepped to one side and raised the machete again. But when I brought it back down, I didn't look at the stump. I looked into Joe 'Neezer's ugly face.

And his face opened wide as he hollered: "Lawd!" He cried out and hopped about and wrung his hands... and Aunt Mattie came to see what happened.

Only then did I look down at the machete and see the blood on the blade. I had chopped right through his shoe, into his foot. I dropped the machete and ran out of the banana patch. 'Neezer squealed like a pig and cried out curse words that if it was me Aunt Mattie would wash out my mouth. But it was me that cut up 'Neezer's foot, and I was afraid of what he might do to me.

I watched from the far side of the pit latrine as Aunt Mattie helped 'Neezer to hobble over to the outhouse. She opened the door and told him to sit inside and stick his cut foot out the door. He sat on the narrow space between the holes and swatted at the flies that pitched about his head. He drew in his breath, sharp and noisily, as Aunt Mattie eased off the shoe and peeled his sock down over the end of his toes. The blood was turning dark already, and was sticking to the sock where the machete had cut through. Three toes were bad, the flesh drawn so you could see the bone. But I knew he wouldn't limp for more than a week or two, that the toes would heal and the bleeding I caused 'Neezer would stop long before he stopped bleeding poor Joshua for his loan. And Aunt Mattie would be the one to pay.

Day in Court

C arol dabbed her neck with a Kleenex. She couldn't feel the gentle stir of air even when she watched the ceiling fan slowly revolve. It hung over the court room and spun with a lazy even rhythm. Its motion did little to cool the crowd sitting shoulder to shoulder on the benches.

Carol had chosen to sit in the last row, by a window, because she thought it would be more comfortable there. But the window sill was bleached by the mid-morning sun. She sat wedged between an elderly man in a dark suit and a plump black woman in a bright pink polyester dress, and beyond the reach of the fan's soft breeze.

For a brief moment she wished she had taken Bertram's advice. If she had, she wouldn't be here, searching her handbag for another tissue to wipe fresh sweat from her face while she waited for her case to be called.

"It's just five hundred dollars, for Christ sake," Bertram had said. "For five hundred, you want to suffer through Small Claims Court? It's different here, you know."

"It's the principle that matters," Carol had said, defensively. "Besides it might be an interesting experience - Small Claims Court Jamaica-style."

"Not one you'll enjoy, I can tell you from now." Bertram had thrown his hands up in the air in a gesture of exasperation. "I'll never understand you Canadians."

He had been unable to convince Carol that suing Rosco Harris was more trouble than it was worth. She was determined to go through with it. After all, it had been Rosco who had reversed his big Chevy into her little VW, so she felt he should pay for the damage.

Carol squirmed, pushing away the dark-suited leg on one side and the thick arm with the pink frill of sleeve on the other, re-establishing her space on the bench. The hushed mumble that had accompanied the court proceedings was suddenly replaced by a commotion. As the noise of chatter grew louder, grey-suited men got up from the table at the front of the room and left, to be replaced by other grey-suited men.

The judge frowned as he wrote in the large book open in front of him. Then he looked up and nodded at the Clerk of the Court standing beside his desk. The Clerk called out, "Brownley versus Jarvis".

A short white-haired man in a soiled grey-blue suit stood in front of the lawyers' table and outlined the conflict in the next case. It had something to do with a dispute over land being used for a chicken farm.

"So this property belongs to one Theo Brownley?" asked the judge.

"Yes, Your Honor, but he died intestate and the eldest son, Mr. George Brownley, took charge of the land." The man in the grey-blue suit wiped his hands on the pockets of his jacket.

"And the chicken farm, it predates the passing of Mr. Theo Brownley?"

"Yes, Your Honor."

At this rate, Carol thought the case was going to take a long time. She shifted on the bench again, easing the pressure of the plump woman's hip and the old man's knee. That's how she felt about her relationship with Bertram, caught between the comfortable habit of his company and a growing dissatisfaction.

Somehow it was fitting that they should have met at the squash club, vying for the last of the orange juice at the bar. Their relationship resembled their game: just when she thought she was getting closer, he would hit a boastful corner shot and throw her game. They spent evenings bouncing ideas around, too quickly to be more than a conversation of quips and sallies. At first she had found them amusing, a change of pace from her students' chatter, and her colleagues' complaints. But her attempts to become more personal with Bertram had been met with sarcasm and evasion.

She had been on her way to meet Bertram when the accident happened. She had gone home to change after work and then set out for the club early for their five o'clock court booking. It was a short drive to the club. A big American car had passed her noisy VW beetle; someone inside was shouting and waving a dark arm out the window. When the car drew in front of her, she saw that the greeting had been directed at a man walking on the other side of the road.

A moment later, the car pulled halfway off the road and stopped. Carol stopped her VW behind it. The car, a metallic green Chevy, still took up half the road and an approaching truck took up the other lane. She checked her rear view mirror for traffic and shifted the gears, ready to move off when the truck had passed. Suddenly the Chevy started backing toward her. She tried to reverse, but realized it would be too late to get out of the way. She honked her horn and shouted "Hey, look out!"

The crunch on metal and glass was a shock to her, even though she had watched it happen. The impact jolted her and the VW's engine stalled. She wrenched open the door and almost hit the driver of the Chevy in her haste to get out.

"What di rass yuh doing dere, lady?" Rosco Harris had grabbed the door before it hit him.

"What do you mean, what am I doing? How could you reverse into me? You blind, or too stupid to look where you're backing?" Carol felt her skin redden with anger.

They had exchanged more insults before swapping names and phone numbers. The damage to the VW's fender and headlight wasn't bad enough to stop her driving on to the squash club. She heard glass tinkle against metal as she pulled out into the road. By the time she reached the carpark, she was late enough to expect Bertram to be annoyed. And he was.

"If you're going to be late, at least you could call," he had shouted at her as he walked briskly from the clubhouse door to his own car.

"I couldn't," she shouted back. "I had an accident - and not a convenient phone booth in sight."

Bertram, in his anger, had been so intent on leaving, it took him a moment to realize that Carol was referring to her car. He would be punctual for their squash games, yet he had often been late coming to see her, rarely turning up at her door when he said he would. And he never had an explanation; just a "Got held up", and a shrug of his shoulders when she expressed annoyance.

"Well, it's too late to play a full game now." Bertram bent down to inspect the damage to the VW's headlight.

"Take it to my friend, Jimmy. He'll fix it for a good price."

And that's all he had said about the accident, until she had told him of her plan to sue Rosco Harris for the repairs that his insurance agent refused to cover. The story Rosco had told her was that because his car had suffered from a rear end collision, it must be Carol's fault, so the insurance company would not pay. Then Bertram had told her to forget it, that it wasn't worthwhile.

Carol hoped her case would be next. Bertram was right about one thing. It was uncomfortable in the court room. The heat, the hard bench and the close proximity of sweating bodies became more unpleasant and harder to ignore as the morning wore on.

"So you took charge of the property when your father died, Mr. Brownley?" the judge asked the fat bald man standing in the witness box.

"Yes, sah, Your Honah", he answered. "I is di eldest and responsible, sah."

"Yuh tell dem, George", cried a woman who sat on one of the front benches. "Yuh tell dem how it go."

"Please Miss... Do not interrupt the court proceedings." The judge tried to silence the woman.

"Maizie Brownley, sah," the woman replied. "Your Honah, I is him wife, sah."

"Very well, Mrs. Brownley. Let us continue," said the judge. "Now I understand that the chicken farm was established on the property in dispute before your father died. Is that correct?"

"Yes, sah."

"So why do you want the chicken farm removed from the land now?" asked the lawyer.

"De wife say it stink, sah", said the fat bald man on the stand. "Dem don't care di property, sah, and it stink."

Maizie Brownley jumped up. "Is a disgrace, Your Honah. A disgrace!"

The judge nodded and waved her to sit down. Then he addressed the man on the stand. "How long has the chicken farm been on the land?"

"Not long, sah. Ten, twelve years."

"And the smell only recently became a problem?" asked the lawyer.

"So di wife say, sah." Brownley took a handkerchief out of a pocket and wiped his hands.

"And do you have plans for the land?" asked the judge.

"Not at the present, Your Honah." Brownley wiped the top of his head and his face, then put the handkerchief away.

The judge paused to write in his book. The rumble of chatter grew louder. Carol noticed two women on the bench in front of her. One was young and pretty. The older woman wore a head-tie covering her hair.

"You hear him?" asked the younger woman. "No waan di land fi notten. So is just cussidness mek him waan throw Ezra and di chickens out a street."

The older woman sucked her teeth, "Chu, is fi pure spite."

"But why Uncle George waan spite me? What mi do him?"

"No, is me dem waan spite." The older woman tugged at her head-tie. "Maizie vex because Papa did love me di best. Him gi mi plenty tings before him dead, furnitures and money and di like. Tings she did want fi George and her pickney."

"Den what done, no done?"

"Yes, but she no waan any a di land to come to me nor mine."

"Mi understand." The younger woman nodded. "I is you daughter. Dat's di quarrel." She took her mother's hand. "Mi glad you reach fi today."

"Now Mrs. Brownley," the lawyer had moved to stand in front of Maizie Brownley in the witness box. "When did the smell from the farm become a problem?"

"It always stink, sah."

"But did it get worse recently?"

"Yes, sah. Dem no clean out di place at all, sah, and it stink someting terrible."

The woman in the head-tie jumped up. "Is a lie. She say dat fi spite, Your Honah!"

The judge picked up his gavel and hit his desk with a loud crack. "Sit down and be quiet!"

"But is true, Your Honah!" The younger woman called out. "I keep di place clean. Is lie dem a tell you!"

The court room audience erupted in argument. Above the noise were the shouts of Mrs. Brownley and her sister-in-law. They screamed at each other, "You lie!" and then, "Spite, wicked spite!"

The judge pounded out a persistent beat with his gavel. "Quiet in the court!" And a moment later, "Officer!"

Policemen started to clear the court room, to pull outside the men and women who had left their seats to join in the dispute. Both of Carol's neighbours had pushed and shoved her about in their excitement. The plump woman in pink had cuffed Carol on the ear with her elbow and the old man trampled on her feet, knocking her with his bony knees in his hurry to curse at a man in brown-plaid trousers who waved at everyone and shouted something Carol did not understand.

Soon the court room was half-empty, and the women had stopped shouting. The judge's gavel hammered the desk top once more and the chatter quietened to a mumble.

"There appears to be more to this dispute than the land." The judge motioned the lawyers to confer with him. Their voices weren't loud enough for the people on the benches to hear what they said. When the lawyers returned to their table, the judge said, "The case of Brownley versus Jarvis will be adjourned so that the parties can sort out the real nature of the dispute - and hopefully save the court's time."

It was Carol's turn to shove her way out of the courtroom. The midday sun was fierce, but the warm air outside smelled of freshly cut grass. She walked briskly toward the cafe on the corner. As she got closer she could hear the buzz of flies. They pitched on her and then left for the scraps of food on the sidewalk. She could smell the coconut oil frying as she stepped into the restaurant, and decided not to have french fries with her hamburger.

She had one of those orange malts that Bertram liked. He had very unsophisticated taste - not what she had expected when she first met him in his trendy-labelled squash togs. It was not often that she had seen him in anything else. Their relationship revolved around the squash club. And her apartment, always her apartment and never his; and always his plans for their time together.

Her case would be called after lunch. She was nervous and wished Bertram could be there to give her moral support. But then he hadn't been very supportive the evening of the accident.

Carol put down her half-eaten burger. What was she doing with this man, anyway? She tried to make a mental pros and cons list of their relationship. By the time she had finished her lunch, she had thought of half a dozen reasons to stop seeing Bertram, and only one in his favour. Not a good enough score.

After lunch, Carol's case was called first. She stood in the witness box and told the judge what had happened, pausing frequently so he would write it down. Rosco Harris questioned her, making much of the fact that she hadn't reported the accident to the police until the next afternoon.

"It happened in the evening," she answered. "I didn't want to break the law by driving around without one headlight. And the next day, I had to work until the afternoon."

It was Rosco's word against hers that she had stopped her car before Rosco reversed. But when she asked him about the lawnmower he had been carrying in the open trunk of his car, she knew the suit had swung in her favour.

"Are you seriously telling us that you could see this lady's car behind you, with your car trunk open like that?" asked the judge.

"I had di side mirror, Your Honor."

"But did you use it?" asked Carol. "Or were you too busy looking for your friend on the other side of the road?"

"I know how to drive, lady." Rosco frowned in anger. "Is you dat come so close up behind me."

"What difference would it make how close she was when she stopped?" asked the judge.

"I could a stop before di accident happen, Your Honor," replied Rosco.

"I see." The judge bent over his big book and made notes.

Bertram joined her at the club for a drink to celebrate.

He seemed genuinely glad that Carol had won her case, but said, "I doubt you'll ever actually see the money. The courts won't be too helpful when it comes to collecting."

That was the last negative comment that Carol wanted to hear. She thought about the pros and cons list of her lunch hour.

"Bertram, I think it's time we stopped seeing each other."

"What's the harm in a drink or two between a couple of squash players?" His smile showed uneasiness.

"I've decided I don't want to play with you any more."

Bertram stopped smiling. "Who told you?"

"Told me what?" But Carol didn't need to be told. Somehow she had known all along and had chosen to be ignorant because it was convenient.

"Don't be coy. It doesn't suit you." Bertram frowned. "Did someone here, at the club, say something?"

"Say what?" Carol decided not to make it easy for him.

"Tell you about Mary", he mumbled.

"Who's Mary?" Carol put her drink down and began to look in her handbag for her car keys.

"My wife, of course." Bertram reached forward as if to take her hand. "How did you find out?"

"You just told me."

That Last Day

Mattie sucks her teeth as she pulls at her hair, unravelling the plait she had pinned up early in the morning. Waking late, she'd tucked her hair under her stiff white cap and run across the yard in the dawn gloom to get Mass Johnny's breakfast. Her hair is loose now, and it sticks out around her face.

She takes a firm hold of her hair as she parts it with her wide tooth comb and plaits it again. She can't go out with it so untidy. Not today. Not with Vernon leaving.

That last day with Victor, twelve long years ago, had started early too. Mattie had plaited her hair tight and pretty that morning. And her ribbons matched the blue of her favourite dress. She had tied a fresh apron over her full skirt and hurried out into the clear morning air that smelled of the red earth still wet from the rain of the night before. The sun winked at her from the droplets on the standpipe. And the water was cool and sweet.

She'd felt happy enough to smile. But deep in her heart a sadness burned that would stay with her all day.

She had just sent the younger children off to school when Victor came to the door. He leaned up against the door frame in his cool way.

"So how's Miss Mattie dis morning?" he asked her. The toothpick in his mouth moved from side to side.

"Morning, Victor." Even on that last day she felt shy with Victor. She patted her ribbons and took off her apron. "Yuh coming out wid me den?" Victory shifted his weight and put out his hand to support himself as he leaned on the other side of the door. Mattie loved to watch him move like that; slow and cool, like a dog going to sit down.

"Yes, Ah coming. Ah just have to tidy."

Mattie reaches under the washstand for her face powder, but today it isn't in its usual place. She squats down and peers into the cabinet. That boy Vernon is forever moving things. At least, with him away at school, she will find her things where she put them. But she will miss his toothy grin and clever jokes. He had grown so since he came to live with her at Mass Johnny's. Now he is going to that boarding school, thanks to the scholarship. And with a little help from Mass Johnny, the boy will have a chance to get a good desk job. He won't grow up to be a common labourer like his father.

Her best old dress is a little tight now, but today it's important she look good. Mattie tugs the blue fabric over her hips. Then she looks into the open suitcase. It is filled with Vernon's khaki shirts and brown socks, and the prayer book from Miss Emma sits on top of the new clothes. Mattie wonders if she will know this young boy in his smart uniform, just as she had hardly recognized him when he first came to live with her at Mass Johnny's. That's when she first thought she should tell him the truth. But he was only seven years old, and wouldn't understand why his grandma had told him his mother was a dead sinner who left him in her care. So she didn't tell him then; she told him to call her "Auntie".

As they walked down the street that last morning, Victor and Mattie could hear the hard slap of dominoes on a tabletop. It came from the group of old men squatting on orange boxes outside the rum shop. That's what happened to old men when they were too feeble to dig yam hills and cut bananas. Victor wanted more for himself and he was leaving that night to find a better life. The farm work in America was just the beginning.

But that last day he was still with her, still holding her hand and walking her out to the countryside, past the school that rang with the shouts of children reciting their lessons. He laughed and called out the lesson with the children. "Tree times tree make nine!" he cried, prancing around like a little boy.

He looked so funny, Mattie couldn't help but laugh and call out too, "Four times four...!"

But she stopped laughing when they reached the church. Her heart sank in her chest so quickly, she clapped her hand over her mouth so she wouldn't cry out. She looked down and watched her feet kick up dust as she passed the big wooden door.

As long as she could remember she had gone to church on Sundays. Her father was an elder in the church, her mother a member of the Altar Guild. Church and preaching and the Christian life meant more to her family than to most people in that town. They would never understand what had happened. And Mattie didn't know how she was going to tell them. She didn't know how to tell Victor either.

When they reached the open land just beyond the coffee piece, the grass was still damp with morning dew. Mattie thought it smelled as sweet as that evening earlier in the summer when they had left the church supper to walk out in the full moonlight. They had sat under that cotton tree at the corner of the field, laughing and touching and holding each other, hidden there in the curve of the roots of the big old tree.

Victor took her hand and began to run across the field, high stepping through the tall grass. Mattie held tight to his strong fingers and tried to keep up with him but he was too fast. She tripped and felt herself falling, but he turned back and pulling her into his arms, lifted her off her feet and swung her around, laughing in her face, now high above him.

Then he put her down and kissed her, but it wasn't right, out there in the field for all to see. He took her hand again as they walked slowly to the cotton tree and sat in the curve of the root, in their special place. He touched her and kissed her and held her like he had that night. But when his hands reached into her dress, she said, "No."

"But we not going do notten we don't do before."

Mattie shook her head, "No."

"I just going love yuh, baby."

"Is broad daylight, Victor. We can't do dat now," she said. "Not here."

"Nobody going to see us."

Maybe that's when she should have told him, but she couldn't. She couldn't say the words and have him curse her. Not with him so close, touching her, his fingers so gentle. So she helped him with the buttons.

Mattie snaps the locks shut on the suitcase and lifts it to the floor by the door. She hears Vernon on the step outside.

"Time to go fi di bus, Aunt Mattie," he calls.

"Di grip is by di door," she calls back. She looks under the bed for her good shoes. They pinch her feet so she only wears them when she thinks people will notice. She wipes the dust off with the heel of her hand and eases her feet into them with the help of a piece of Vernon's old ruler. She tucks a well-worn handbag under her arm and opens the door.

"See it there? Pick up di grip and make haste." She immediately regrets her tone of voice. After all, he will be on the bus soon enough, and away until Christmas. He shouldn't remember her as so cross.

Vernon reaches in with arms that look as if they are long for his body, and he pulls out the suitcase. It is too heavy for him to carry on his head, and it almost touches the ground as he walks out the gate and up the hill to the bus stop, with Mattie behind him.

The boy walks tall and strong for one so young. Eleven years old and smart enough to pass the scholarship exam. Mattie stands straighter with the pride she feels for her boy. But is she proud enough to tell him so today? Or is he still too young and foolish to understand these things?

Mattie reaches out to touch Vernon's brown head, but he moves away, out into the road.

"Is di bus, Aunt Mattie!" She hears the excitement in his voice.

"Is over dere it gwine stop." Vernon points across the road. "Come, before it reach." He picks up the suitcase and hurries across the road to the small group gathered there.

Mattie moves more slowly and waits to let the bus pass her and stop in front of the people waiting for it. When she reaches the far side of the bus, Vernon is already telling the driver to put his suitcase up top with the other people's baggage. She looks at his long thin limbs and thinks maybe she should tell him. But how can she make him understand everything?

She could tell from how quiet he was that last day that Victor was sad too. They walked slowly, stopping to show each other this flower and that tree, like they'd never been that way before. When they reached her door she knew she should tell him. She even opened her mouth to speak but when he turned away and said, "See yuh later, baby," she just nodded and mumbled, "Uh-huh."

Her brothers and sisters came in from school, quarrelling and pushing each other about. She told them to behave, but they mocked her and carried on. Until one of them remembered, "Shush, is today Victor gwine leave her."

But the quiet after that was almost worse than the noise. They settled to their homework and she cooked dinner before she went back into town to see Victor. She had that long to make up her mind, but she couldn't. What if she didn't tell him? Would he still come back? Perhaps not.

It was sunset on that last day when Mattie left the house to go and say goodbye to Victor. Her heart was truly heavy; it sank deeper in her chest with every step into the town. When she got there the bus was already there, the driver up on the roof packing away suitcases and baskets of produce. Two higgler women shouted up at him, telling him to take care of their goods because they couldn't sell anything that spoiled before it reached market.

Victor was there too. He stood watching and waiting his turn to pass up the old borrowed case he held at his side. He put it down when he saw her.

"Hi, baby," he said as he flung his arms open like somebody in a movie. And Mattie ran to him, into those arms. She hugged him and willed him to hold her long and hard.

"Hey, girl. Wah happen?" he asked, as if he wasn't going anywhere at all. "Yuh not going cry, eh baby?"

Mattie lifted her head for him to see the tears that trickled down her cheeks. "Don't go, Victor."

"Cho, we done talk bout dat." He frowned and looked away in anger.

"But yuh cyaan go now," she hugged harder.

He pushed her away. "Don't talk foolishness."

The bus driver leaned down and called to Victor. "Dat case to come up yah?"

Victor picked up his suitcase and tossed it to the driver. Then he turned to Mattie and said, "Yuh see? Mi going."

Mattie said nothing. She dried her cheeks and stood watching her hands play with her handkerchief. The driver soon climbed down from the baggage rack and people from the roadside started to get into the bus.

Victor touched her arm. "Is time, Mattie," he said quietly.

She looked up into his face. There was no anger there, only sadness.

"Ah going to have yuh baby." The words came out of her mouth without her thinking them, like they knew they had to be said.

"Oh God, Mattie. I gwine come back, yuh know." He hugged her close and kissed her. "I gwine come back." Then he left her and got into the bus.

She watched him push his way to a window seat. He leaned out to her and shouted, but the noise of that old bus pulling out into the road was all she could hear.

Mattie opens her old handbag and pushes the things about until she finds a handkerchief. "Come here, bwoy," she calls to Vernon. He comes to her and lets her wipe away dust and milk stains from his face.

"I going to be alright, yuh know, Auntie," he says to her solemn face. "Mi did reach here wid no trouble at all, when Grandma dead."

"Yes, I know." He smile is sad. "And yuh was only a little ting den."

Vernon looks over his shoulder at the other people getting on to the bus. Then he reaches up and kisses her on the cheek. "I gone now, Auntie."

But she holds him and touches his chin so he must look at her. "Vernon."

"Yes, Auntie?"

But the words, they don't pop out of her mouth like they did that last day with Victor. She tries again, "Vernon."

"Hurry, Auntie. Di bus going leave me."

"Behave yuhself, boy. And see dat yuh study hard."

"Yes, Auntie." And he runs to the bus and disappears into the crowd inside.

The old bus belches smoke and dust and pulls out into the road. Mattie watches it turn the corner and pass out of town. She crosses the road. Perhaps the time was wrong after all. Besides, what earthly reason is there for him to know?

Baking

Emma put on a clean apron that morning. It would be dirty with flour and molasses by evening, but a fresh apron was the best she could do to make the day.

The lard in the mixing bowl hadn't softened. She pounded sugar into the lumps of white fat. The vigorous action felt right for her mood. There had been a balloon of sadness in her chest, like heartburn, when she woke that morning and remembered the anniversary. The balloon of pain would deflate slowly as the day wore on, but beating the lard seemed to help.

She pulled the flour bag out from under the pantry counter. "Is not enough fi di bun dem," she mumbled, scooping flour into the sifter.

"Ma'am?" Mattie, the maid, looked up from the sink full of breakfast dishes and soap suds.

"The flour, it don't look like enough fi today."

"Yes, ma'am?"

"Well, go to di shop fi more." Sometimes Mattie's slowness gnawed at Emma's patience.

Once Mattie had left, the house was quiet. Emma's husband, Mass Johnny, had left early for the yam hill; and the children were all at school. The last one would have started school this year, too.

Emma rubbed her neck; the sadness bubble had moved up to her throat. She didn't have time to feel like that - to grieve for a child who had never been born. She had to bake cakes and buns for market, to bring in extra money. The times were hard - had been for six years. At first, the less Johnny got for his crops, the more he wanted her. So she shouldn't have been surprised when she started to get that familiar queasiness in the mornings.

She stood on tiptoe to reach the tin of molasses. As she stirred it in, she watched the mixture in the bowl get darker. There was something about the taste of molasses that reminded her of that last pregnancy. That sweetness would have made her sick to her stomach with the others. Perhaps it would have been a special child. She never found out if it was a boy or a girl.

Maybe it was better that way.

Mattie came through the pantry door, the new bag of flour balanced on her head. "Lawd, Missis. Yuh should hear Winifred Johnstone chatting her business out a street today."

"Mi no waan fi hear it."

"Yes, Ma'am." Mattie put the flour bag next to the old one.

"Grater di coconut."

Mattie started out the door.

"Yuh don't crack di coconut yet?" Emma asked.

"No, Ma'am." Mattie hesitated. "It in di kitchen still."

"Didn't I tell yuh to crack dat coconut from morning?"

Emma thwacked her wooden spoon against the mixing bowl.

"Yes, Ma'am. Soon come wid it, Ma'am." Mattie hurried through the door, a puzzled frown on her face. Emma picked up the spoon again. She added ginger and cinnamon to the mixture, then more flour. She stirred, hugging the bowl to her. Her strokes soon gained speed and rhythm. She quietly counted the strokes: "One, two, three, four... two, three, four... three, four."

No, only three, she had made sure of that. But what else could she have done? There was so little money then. The prices for coffee and bananas were low; and the yams and ginger root were hard to sell. Only her chicken money had been steady. And now the baking; sometimes it brought in extra money - sometimes she didn't sell enough to cover her costs. At least she could feed the stale cornelia cake to her chickens.

Six years ago she couldn't even pay the rent on a stall in the market. They had eaten a lot of yam, and very little bread then. And cake was only for the children's birthdays. Another mouth to feed; it would be too hard. The other children would suffer. As it was they complained about so much yam. They put up with the clumsy shoemaker's sandals, and clothes made from feed sacks. It wouldn't be right to take from them for another baby. The last pregnancy was a mistake; what else could she have done about it?

Johnny was happy when he saw the first signs. He loved the children and didn't think about the hardship. After all, he saw them fed every night and clothed every morning. How could he know how she managed that? She would take the few dollars he gave her and add her own egg money. But she couldn't stretch it for one more baby; she knew it. She had felt a familiar joy with the nausea that first day. But just as she sensed the changes in her body even before they showed, so she also knew that she would have to find a way to end it.

Mattie placed an enamel dish of grated coconut on the counter beside the mixing bowl.

"Thank yuh." Emma began to mix the flakes into the bowl. "Yuh did get di oven ready?"

Mattie nodded. "Time fi di larger pans?" She took down the large baking sheets from on top of the screened food cupboard.

Emma poured the cake dough into the pans. "Alright. Go on wid dat. I'll bring dis last one."

Mattie carried the larger of the cakes out to the kitchen. Emma scraped the mixing bowl clean and spread the batter evenly in the pan. She carried the cake pan the short distance to the kitchen outside. When she entered the small, soot-darkened room, she saw the bright flames in the old wood and coal stove.

"Di stove not ready at all!"

"Yuh know it tek time, Miss Emma." Mattie poked at the wood burning in the grate. "Cho, it soon ready, ma'am. No bodder yuhself bout it."

"And di day soon done, too - and market tomorrow." Emma slammed the cake pan on the table by the door and turned to leave.

"What a trouble yuh, Miss Emma?" Mattie mumbled.

Emma heard her, but didn't answer. She didn't know what she could tell this woman who had worked beside her all these years. She returned to the pantry and started sifting flour for the buns. The lard was softer this time and blended with the sugar quickly and evenly. She soon had the dough ready to roll out. She floured the counter and started to knead. Then she rolled out the dough and added the sugar and cinnamon. She folded it until it was ready to be cut into the circle shaped buns.

The children used to love helping with these buns. Back then little hands would roll strips of dough to mimic the spiral of the buns. Each child had taken a turn standing on the chair to reach across the counter to the mixing bowl. Later she would have to wash flour from their faces, hair, and up to their elbows. They were so cute at that age that she would stop her work to hug and play with them. The youngest had started school two years ago. Baking day hadn't been the same since.

Emma watched the gentle motion of her hands rolling and drawing out the dough. She would have loved that child, held it close to her and felt the softness of its skin against her cheek, its little arms clasped around her neck. It wasn't that she had not wanted the child: she would have not known how to feed it once her milk was gone.

"Mattie, weh di baking sheets fi di buns?"

"Coming, Ma'am."

Mattie helped her fill the sheets with the round medallions of dough. Then she carried them out to the stove.

Emma wiped off the counter. The first batch were in the oven. Sure that she would have something for the stall tomorrow, she could take a break. She took a heel of sugar bun and a piece of cheese from the screened cupboard. She sat at the dining table, her feet resting on the rungs of the next chair. She sighed as she felt the blood rush down into her feet. The dull ache was soothing. But the pain she had been remembering all day hadn't been so easily dulled.

Emma had put off thinking about the baby for weeks. She had put off making a decision, hoping nature would solve her problem. It had happened before, a miscarriage early in a pregnancy. But when time passed and nothing happened, she knew she would have to slip through the coffee piece into Miss Annie's place. That spry old woman knew about "science". A couple of draughts of potion from the doctor shop and it would all be over. At least, that's what Miss Annie had told her.

But three days later Emma was in hospital, bleeding so badly that she knew something had gone very wrong. It had begun with a twinge of pain. It wasn't until she fainted that her eldest daughter saw the blood and ran screaming out to the field for her father. The pain and the blood got worse even in the hospital. She knew the baby was gone, but so were parts of her insides. The doctor said it was because the miscarriage had happened so late in the pregnancy.

For weeks Emma was too weak to walk, and too sad to say anything to Johnny about it. She cried when she saw the useless milk leaking from her swollen breasts. She felt guilty and sorry for what she had done, even though she still knew she had no real choice. And she felt guilty that she was unable to cook for the children.

That was when Mattie came to them. At first she cooked and cleaned in exchange for a room and a share of the yams. When there was a little to spare, Mass Johnny paid her pocket money. Later she would get a share of the cake and egg money; she would become part of the family.

Emma stood up and brushed the crumbs off the table into her hand. She washed her fingers at the pantry sink, then started to make another bowl of cake batter.

The pantry door slammed behind Mattie. She put the sheets of baked cake and buns on the counter. She began cutting the cake into squares.

"Look good today, Miss Emma."

"What I tell yuh?" Emma's voice was sharp and loud. "Don't cut dem so big. Can't mek money if yuh give it away."

"Mi know, Ma'am. How many I cut from I come?" Mattie paused as if expecting another rebuke. "Is six years, yuh know, Ma'am. Six years since yuh fall so sick, and I come to help wid di children and ..." Mattie stopped suddenly. She looked at Emma for a moment, then cut another section of cake.

The two women worked in silence, cutting cake squares and separating cinnamon buns. Mattie wrapped each portion in waxed paper and set them in layers in baskets. Emma went back to mixing cake batter. Mattie washed and oiled the baking sheets; Emma poured the batter, spreading it out evenly with the back of her wooden spoon. The mornings's routine was repeated, and the bubble of sadness slowly shrank in her chest. Emma noticed that Mattie began to anticipate the next step. She tried to apologize for her sharp tongue of that morning. She didn't know what to say to a woman who had come to her when she was little more than a child. So she said nothing.

It was late in the evening when Emma finished preparing the last of the cinnamon buns. She took the sheet of doughy spirals out to the kitchen. She opened the stove to check on the fire. She stirred the glowing embers and felt the heat on her face. Her eyes burned, a tear escaping onto her cheek. She sniffed and closed the stove. She wiped her cheek, and turned to see Mattie coming through the door. Emma stood up, stretched her tired back and said, "Well, di day soon done."

Mattie looked at Emma for a moment before she smiled and said, "Yes, Ma'am." She reached out and touched her arm. "Is alright, yuh know, Miss Emma. yuh and I know how tings stay."

Darrell's Bicycle

Darrell fingers the keys in his pocket and kicks at the tire. It is flat, a shiny new hubcap with a flat tire: that's his kind of luck.

Darrell shrugs his shoulders and leans forward to touch the shiny fender of his car. He had saved for a long time for this beauty. Darrell smiles at how the sleek, deep wine red Ford looks out of place parked in the middle of the farmyard in the mountains of Jamaica. So it should, he thinks. It belongs to the life he will make for himself in Kingston - not to the one he will leave behind here.

"Yuh going to fix dat deh flat tire, bwoy?" His mother's voice is clear and loud as she calls to him from the verandah.

"Yes, Mama."

His reply is little more than a mumble. He turns away and strolls to the back of the car, jingling the keys in his hand. He opens the trunk and stands looking at the space, empty since he took out his suitcase that morning. There are no tools in sight. The spare tire is well hidden too. He bends over to pull the mat aside. The just-new smell tickles his nostrils. He loves that smell.

He can't remember having anything this new before. Even the only bicycle he had as a boy was a hand-me-down. When his cousin Horace moved with his family to Kingston, Darrell was left the bicycle.

It was a funny looking bicycle; the tires were smaller than most, narrower too. But it was his, and he rode it everywhere until he got one too many flats and had to take it to the shop across from the church to ask Mr. Braddock to fix it. The patching job was difficult because there had been many before and Mr. Braddock suggested that it was time to purchase a new tire.

One was ordered, but they didn't make that size anymore. When his mother found out she insisted that Darrell put the bicycle away, to use it only "for important errands and the like." But Darrell loved riding his bicycle so he would sneak out with it now and then when his parents weren't around.

The tire went flat again, and because he wasn't supposed to have been riding the bicycle, he took the tires off and hid them.

One Saturday, when his parents had left for market, he couldn't resist the temptation to take out the bicycle to ride it about on the rims alone, around and around on the patch of grass in front of the house. As he went around, he picked up speed until he was going fast enough to take his feet off the pedals and tuck them up on the cross bar. But he had trouble steering the bicycle like that. He lost control and careened into the fence. When he got up and tried to straighten out the bicycle he found he couldn't. The front rim was so badly bent that when he stood on it and pulled, it only became a stranger shape. Then he tried to wheel the bicycle back to the house and discovered that he had damaged the axle.

He circled the bicycle for a while, trying to figure out what to do. He found a wrench and a screwdriver in his father's tool box and sat on the back steps and carefully dismantled the bicycle, piece by piece. He then searched for a place to hide it. He knew that the fowlhouse was too small and full of things like buckets and egg baskets that people used every day. And everyone knew that under the house was his place, so that wouldn't leave room for him to blame anybody else. Finally, he decided that it would have to be hidden in the house, some place where no one ever looked, like under a bed or on top of a cupboard.

Darrell finds the jack in the trunk. As he kneels down by the offending tire, he tugs at his trouser legs and the feel of the new fabric stops him. It's bad enough that his brand new car gets a flat tire, he doesn't want to ruin his new coming-home trousers too... He had bought this suit with what was left of his scholarship money. It was from a discount house, but no one need know; as long as he looked like the smart, mature man he had become while at college in Canada.

He looks across the front verandah, with its wood fretwork border now broken in odd places. The old rose-apple tree is still there, on the far side. He starts toward it before he remembers that there wouldn't be any dried banana leaves there now that his father has sold the mules and drays. He will have to look for something else to kneel on.

When he was a little boy, there were always big dried banana leaves and trash under the rose-apple tree, dumped from the mule drays kept parked in front of the house. His father used to send bananas to the train at Kendal in those two wheeled wooden carts that always looked so silly when they stood empty and tilted without a mule tied up in the shafts. Darrell used to climb the rose-apple tree and sit nibbling the thin flesh on the big rose-apple seeds. When he had eaten all the fruit he could reach, he would jump down into the pile of banana trash. Some days he would climb and jump until the banana trash was spread all over the front yard, into his mother's rosebeds and even on the verandah. Then his mother would yell at him and tell him to "stop dat noise and clean up di mess."

"Is weh yuh have di crocus bag dem?" he calls out to whoever can hear him in the house.
"Is what yuh want wid a crocus bag, bwoy? Is dat yuh going tek fix di tire, eh?" His mother's cackle of a laugh taunts him.
"Cho, just tell me weh di bag dem deh, nuh."
"In di old fowlhouse."
Darrell strides towards the wattle and thatch hut on the other side of the farmyard. It must be the oldest building on this land. The wooden shelves of roosting nests for the hens are still firmly attached to the plastered walls... He had often helped his mother collect eggs here, from under hens who squawked in protest. And one day he had snuck in here alone to watch a hen stand and flap her wings as she strained and puck-pucked her egg into her nest. He had laughed, thinking the bird was going to pass a large turd. Later, he came to understand that chickens left the small, wet droppings

in the yard. Now the old hen roosts are full of kerosene pans and old enamel wash basins, bashed up ewer jugs and buckets that have lost their handles.

On the lower shelf the crocus bags are piled haphazardly. Darrell picks up one and walks back to the car. Out of habit, he stops to check the ground for fresh, smelly chicken shit before spreading the bag beside the flat tire. As he kneels down he looks up to see the new fowlhouse, its large structure of wooden pillars and open chicken wire around roosts for the hens, and he realizes that they no longer roam the farmyard.

"Hey, Darrell!" his mother calls from the verandah. "Yuh going get dat tire fix in time to tek Mattie out to di clinic?"

"What time she have to be there?"

"Two-thirty."

"Yes, alright."

"At least di boasy car good fi someting."

Darrell could hear his mother's cackle, and the giggles of his sisters, Esmie and Bea. Even the cook, Mattie, must be laughing.

He had always felt left out, outnumbered as the only boy. Now that he was back from college, he hoped he would get some respect as the eldest, the traveller, the educated one. But instead he felt like he had that summer's evening on campus when he had referred to the winking lights in the tall grass as peeny wallies. His companions had burst out laughing, mocking him and clutching their crotches suggestively. His first months in Canada had been difficult because he spoke English and was fair-skinned like the Canadians, so they expected him to know the same things they did. But he didn't know about snow and ice then or about what things were called, like with the fireflies. But as he learned to speak with less of a Jamaican accent, and to bundle up for the cold, he began to forget those early humiliations.

Coming home to the familiar giggles of his sisters brought back feelings that were buried deeper. Yet they still burned. Like the memory of the day that he decided to go with Esmie to her music lesson. His going had something to do with music lessons being for girls and so a source of mystery to him. Besides, it was raining and Esmie didn't want to go alone. He had followed Esmie up the hill to Miss Rowena's little house, where the upright piano took up half of the drawing room, so that he couldn't sit there unnoticed during the lesson. He had sat on the verandah and listened to Esmie struggle through some classical piece.

The lesson seemed to take forever, and he began to feel an urge to relieve himself. The lesson continued until he became uncomfortable and began to pace along the verandah, peering over the sides in the hope of seeing an outhouse in the back. It was raining harder, and the drips of water from the eves made him more uncomfortable. It got so he could either relieve his bladder over the side of the verandah, or wet himself. He turned his back to the sound of the piano and leaned against the railing. He hoped that the slats of the verandah railing and the rain would camouflage what he planned to do. But as he turned back toward the sound of Esmie's piano playing, and pulled up his zipper, he heard a shout. Miss Rowena stood at the door, drawn to her full height.

"Darrell!" she shouted again. "What yuh been doing, bwoy?"

"Notten, ma'am." His hands had frozen at his crotch as if to betray his guilt.

"Don't tell me notten, boy." And she strode over to

him and pushed him against the railing. "You're a rude, vulgar child. I can't believe dat yuh fine mother would bring yuh up so!"

"Ma'am?"

"Now, since yuh so like to play wid dat zip, yuh can drop dem pants so I can beat yuh."

He turned toward the railing, undid his belt and let his shorts drop.

"Take that, and that!" she said as she thwacked his bottom with a ruler. The first one didn't hurt, but she kept striking him harder. His bottom became tender until tears came to his eyes, and he started to sniffle to stop his nose from running.

"You're a rude, rude boy!" she shouted over the sound of the ruler slapping his bottom.

Then the piano went silent and Esmie came out to the verandah. She laughed at him and asked, "What yuh did, Darrell?"

"Well, that's enough," said Miss Rowena, saving both of them the embarrassment of explaining to Esmie. "You'd best take dis rude boy home now... and see that yuh don't bring him back here." And with that Miss Rowena stomped into her drawing room and slammed the door.

Esmie had got the details she had missed by torturing him with slaps on his sore bottom. By the time they got home she was laughing so hard it took her several minutes to calm herself enough to tell the family what had happened. Bea started to giggle even before the whole story was out and his mother had scowled a "Yuh got what yuh deserve" before her laugh broke up her frown.

He had taken refuge under the house, in the space below the back steps. That was his place, like the rose-apple tree had been when he was younger. It had given him a sense of belonging when his sisters' giggles made him an outsider.

"Yuh soon finish, boy?" His mother's voice taunts him again. "If Mattie have to walk, she must go now."

"Yes, I'll be ready in good time."

"Well, I hope dat yuh change in all di time yuh spend in a Canada. Yuh know, yuh and time never used to tek to one anodder."

Darrell puts on the last of the wheel lugs and gets up to stomp on the socket wrench to tighten it. He tightens each lug in turn. Then he bends over to take up the shiny hubcap and dusts it off with the crocus bag before replacing it on the wheel.

He draws the crocus bag across the fender. He is proud of his new car, and it will always be called "Darrell's car". Not like the bicycle; it was always referred to as "Horace's bicycle".

"Yuh not finish yet?" His mother stands at the door.

"Yes, Ah coming now."

Darrell throws the crocus bag over the verandah railing and pushes by his mother to go into the house. He begins to wash just his hands, but in the cool of the house he can feel his shirt sticking to him. He washes away the sweat from working in the midday sun. Taking the damp shirt with him, he goes into his room and finds a clean one in the old wardrobe that had been moved from the girls' room. It shakes as he shuts the door. The rattling sound is from more than just the hangers inside. He pulls a chair over and steps up onto the seat. He peers into the space behind the old fashioned false front on the wardrobe to see the dismantled bicycle, rusty, but all there.

Obeah Woman

The door slammed behind her. Esmie cried out, the loud whack frightened her. It was louder than the rapid tap of her feet on the wooden verandah. She stumbled on the steps in her rush to get to the street. Then the catch on the low picket gate wouldn't open. She pulled and tugged at it, but she couldn't make it work. The gate stayed shut.

Esmie climbed onto the gate and jumped. Her body smacked the ground. For a moment she lay twisted and sprawled on the path. She scrambled to her feet, hurriedly brushing dirt from her elbows and a grazed knee. She looked back up at the door. It was still closed.

She could see Miss Rowena standing inside, watching her through the screen. Esmie couldn't make out the woman's face, only the dark shape of her body. She had run out of the little house so quickly, she hadn't seen her piano teacher's anger. She didn't wait to see the woman step onto the verandah. Esmie was running down the street when she heard her name.

"Esmie. Wait, child. Esmie!" Miss Rowena ran

down the steps and called again from the gate. "Esmi..ee!
Is wah happen to dat chile, eeh?

By the time she reached the crossroads, Esmie's
thin white legs hurt, and her knees were shaking. She
waited for a bus to pass her. She looked back; she could
see Miss Rowena still at her gate. Dirt kicked up by the
bus sprayed the child. She ran across the road and
started down the hill.

Esmie couldn't see the concrete pillars that held the
gate to her father's farm. If she reached them, she would
be safe. But she didn't know how she would explain why
she had run away from her piano lesson with Miss
Rowena. Esmie wished she didn't have to say anything,
the way grownups don't. Maybe she could hide until it
was late enough, so they wouldn't wonder why she was
home early.

Esmie reached the steepest part of the hill, the part
just before Mrs. Braddock's place. She slowed down,
afraid of losing her footing, afraid she would fall again
and dirty her dress. Then she would have to tell them
what had happened.

The otaheite apple trees in Mrs. Braddock's yard
had only a few of the red pear-shaped fruit. It was early
in the season so she wouldn't be looking out for children
stealing her apples. Esmie knew those trees, she had
been one of the children Mrs. Braddock had chased out
of her trees last year. It would be safe to hide there until
it was time to go home. She pulled her skirt close about
her legs and stepped through the barbed wire fence at
the side of the widow's house.

Mrs. Braddock liked people to believe that she was
a widow, but even Esmie had heard the rumour that Mr.
Braddock had not died, but had run away to Montego

Bay with a young girl who use to work in Mr. MacCaulay's drygoods shop. No one ever saw Mrs. Braddock go into that shop again. She would send a young man to buy what she needed. She always seemed to have a young man working for her, cutting wood and helping her, even in the house.

Esmie reached for the lowest branch of an otaheite tree. Clasping it firmly, she swung her feet up onto the limb. She climbed high enough so she could see the road and beyond, to Miss Annie's yard.

Mass Johnny, Esmie's father, had sold Miss Annie a piece of land on the corner of his property. He didn't know she was a poco woman then, but once she settled into her little house she had built on the land, she displayed her intentions, flying brightly coloured flags on bamboo poles outside her door; and tying strips of red and white cloth to her fencepost.

Esmie sat among the leaves and watched an old man drive a badly made dray past the gate of her father's farm. The donkey walked slowly, its head hung down almost to the ground. The old man picked up a whip. He threw it back over his shoulder. From where Esmie sat, it looked as if the tip of the whip hit one of the white pillars by the gate. The old man cracked the whip and hit the donkey.

"Gwan, Bumbo!" He swung the whip again. The donkey flinched and picked up his hooves, moving faster as he began to climb the next rise.

Esmie didn't like to see the donkey struggle in pain. Perhaps her father would hit her for leaving her piano lesson. Esmie turned away and saw that from her branch she could watch Mrs. Braddock's young man chopping wood in the backyard. This one wasn't so tall, but Esmie could tell he had a strong back. She watched the muscles ripple on his shoulders as he lifted the axe and split the log set on the stump before him. She couldn't see his face, but knew he would be handsome. Mrs. Braddock's young men were always good looking.

Esmie started to move back along the branch, toward the tree trunk. But she stopped when she saw someone coming out of the back of Mrs. Braddock's house. The woman's house frock was unbuttoned down the front. A lace slip showed when the frock flapped open as she walked. She called the young man's name, "Abel."

As she drew closer Esmie could see that the woman was Mrs. Braddock. She gripped the limb, afraid that the woman would hear her.

Mrs. Braddock stopped Abel's woodcutting. She put a hand on his dark sweat-wet shoulder. She ran her fingers over his back as she said something too softly for Esmie to hear. Abel turned and Esmie saw a smile crease his handsome face. Abel went back to his woodchopping; Mrs. Braddock continued to caress his smooth dark skin. Her brown fingers danced over the ripples of muscle on his back. Then she began to play with the waist of his trousers. Esmie could hear her giggling. The older woman pulled at the fabric of the pants. Then she ran a hand inside them. Abel let go of the axe. It fell onto the stump with a thwack.

"Woman, wah di rass yuh do dat fah?" Abel grabbed Mrs. Braddock about the shoulders with both hands. She laughed and pulled him closer to her. She said something in a soft singsong voice, and they both laughed.

Esmie clung to the branch she sat on and strained forward to watch Abel and Mrs. Braddock walk, arm about each other, to the house. She wondered about the obeah Mrs. Braddock had worked on the good looking young man, Abel. She wondered if Miss Annie knew about this kind of guzu.

Esmie had heard people joke about going to see Miss Annie to get potions to use against an enemy or to attract a lover. She remembered a school mate talking about how her auntie went to Miss Annie to be healed of some sickness. Perhaps Miss Annie knew about the kind of obeah that Miss Rowena had used this afternoon. Esmie wished she could talk to someone who understood these things. But she was afraid of Miss Annie, even though she lived next door.

It was time to go home. On a normal day, her piano lesson would be over and she would be walking down the hill to the gate with the white pillars. Esmie swung down out of the otaheite tree. Her feet hit the ground with a thud. She regained her balance and stepped carefully between the trees toward the barbed wire fence. Behind her she could hear soft cries, whimpering sounds coming from Mrs. Braddock's house. She stopped at the fence. The sounds got louder like the noises she had heard from Miss Annie's when she held a pocomania meeting. There were many things she didn't understand that frightened her. How could she tell her family about what happened that afternoon if she didn't know herself? Esmie climbed through the fence and straightened her dress before she started across the road.

The piano lesson had begun in the same way they had all started, every Thursday afternoon for the past year. Esmie played the pieces she had practised. Miss Rowena made her play one piece faster, the other slower. "Tempo, child, tempo."

Then she had started to teach Esmie a new piece. The fingering was difficult. Miss Rowena showed her how the first few bars should be played. Esmie tried to play so it sounded the same. When she got the fingering wrong, Miss Rowena had taken her hand and moved her fingers to show her. Esmie struggled through the piece and Miss Rowena responded warmly, "That's good. Now try it once more."

Esmie had played the piece again. It sounded more like music. She had got the fingering right most of the time. Miss Rowena put an arm around her shoulders and hugged her. "Yes, girl dat's it." As she hugged Esmie the tips of her fingers brushed against the swell of her breast.

Esmie nodded and started to play the piece again. Esmie wondered why Miss Rowena hugged her. It was so strange, stranger still was the way it made her feel. She was confused and frightened by what she felt.

Suddenly her fingers wouldn't touch the right notes. She fumbled with the keys, watching her fingers tremble because she didn't know where else to look.

Miss Rowena had said something, which Esmie did not hear. She felt this overwhelming desire to leave, and had run from the room, slamming the door to the verandah.

Esmie opened the gate held in place by the white concrete pillars. She stepped through and turned to lock it again. She felt sure that there would be questions, that she must have answers. She wanted to talk about what happened to someone who could help her understand. But she knew she could never really explain her feelings. She had felt strange, frightened, and yet, for a moment, she hadn't wanted Miss Rowena to stop her obeah.

Country Come to Town

"Come out a di kitchen, Papa."

Horace could hear the annoyance in his mother's voice.

"Yuh don't see how much I have to do? And Horace school tings must buy today."

Horace looked up at the kitchen window. From where he stood in the backyard of their new home, he could see his mother and grandfather inside. While he listened to his mother's complaints, he stripped the leaves from a twig of hibiscus bush that grew against the back wall of the house. He pulled and tugged at the green switch until it broke away.

"Me dear, don't distress yuhself so. Cho, mek me tek di boy fi di tings." His grandfather sounded eager.

Horace raised his hand and brought it quickly down in an arc across the hibiscus bush. The switch he held whipped away leaves in its sweep to the ground. He smelled the freshness of the cut leaves. They were scattered among the sparse grassy weeds that covered most of the backyard.

The grass was thick and green at home, on the farm. Horace didn't understand why they couldn't stay there. Yam and coffee weren't hard to grow. And they could have got a calf from Mass Johnny when the cow died. He felt an ache inside when he thought of the house in the mountains, of the orange trees and of bird shooting with his cousin Darrell. That last day, he had spent an hour finding all his treasures buried under the wooden floors of the house.

The new house in Kingston was small and ugly, with its concrete walls and tiled floors that were cold to walk on. And with no space underneath to hide things.

Horace didn't want to go shopping with Grandpa. Last year he had gone on his own. Big boys like him didn't need anybody to buy school things, not back home. But everything was different in Kingston. His mother didn't trust him to go anywhere alone, besides to the school around the corner.

"Yuh serious, Papa?" his mother asked. "Yuh want tek di boy fi him school clothes?"

"Yes, ma'am. I ready fi see dis yah town."

But Horace wasn't ready to show it to him. He threw down the hibiscus switch and ran around to the front of the house. He slid across the shiny tiles of the verandah and tip-toed through the front door, into his parents' bedroom. He dropped to the floor and rolled under the bed. If Grandpa couldn't find him, maybe he would give up, go sit in his old chair and forget about going downtown.

Grandpa knew less about Kingston than Horace. He thought about what Grandpa had called out as they drove into the city in a car packed to its limits with boxes and suitcases. He pointed at a traffic light and laughed, "Hey, ku moon pon tick!"

Horace's father had looked away from the street

ahead to see where Grandpa was pointing. He laughed and winked at Horace. "No, man. Is electric light dat."

"Horace." He heard Grandpa calling him outside. "Horace!" The old man came around the side of the house. "Horace, weh yuh is, bwoy?"

The click of the old man's boots sounded loud to Horace.

"Boy, yuh in dere?"

He hugged the surface of the tiles, colder in the darkness under the bed. He didn't want to move but his skin began to tingle and itch, in his hair, on his elbow, on the sole of his left foot. He held his breath and resisted the urge to scratch, waiting for his grandfather to move away from the bedroom door.

The click of boots echoed across the floor and Horace let his breath out and reached to scratch his foot with one hand, his elbow with the other. He twisted under the bed, knocking the boxsprings, kicking at the fringe on the bedspread.

"Is what yuh a do dere, boy?"

He quickly flattened himself against the tiles, but it was too late. "Notten, Grandpa." He slid along the floor until he thought he was clear of the bed. He bent his knees to get up and lifted the bed off the floor with his bottom, then fell onto his stomach.

"What yuh mean, notten?"

Horace pushed himself further out into the room. "Mi looking fi someting..."

"In yuh madda bedroom?"

"Yes, is some money mi drop here."

"Oh?" Grandpa chuckled. "So yuh getting ready fi go buy school tings?"

"Weh?"

"To di shops, bwoy."

"Yes, Grandpa." Horace knew it wouldn't help to argue with him.

It was almost midday before they left the house, the September heat heavy in the air. Grandpa stepped into the street like an old soldier on parade, firm strides with the thump of his cane.

Horace's shirt was already sticking to his back. He kicked at tufts of grass on the side of the road while they waited for the bus. Dust covered his crepe-soled shoes, and sank through the lace holes and under the canvas tongue to spread into his socks, the grit rubbing into his feet.

When the bus came, Grandpa stood fumbling with the change in his pocket for so long the driver called out to him: "Yuh coming, ole man?"

Grandpa took the coins out of his pocket. "Please, sah, how much di fare?"

"When las yuh tek bus, grandpa?" The bus driver, and half the passengers in the bus laughed.

"Longer dan yuh live, sah," Grandpa shook his fist full of coins at the driver.

The boy's face burnt with embarrassment. "Grandpa, give me di money."

"Wah fah?" But he opened his hand so the boy could take the right change from it. Horace ran up the steps and was settled into a seat at the back before his grandfather could manage to climb into the bus.

"Now is hurry yuh waan hurry," Grandpa chuckled as he made his way slowly down the length of the bus.

Horace hoped he wouldn't sit beside him, at least not until they had passed the big school. Some of the boys might be playing on the cricket pitch and see him.

The first week of school, he had been careful not to mention the farm. He knew from his visits to Kingston in the past that the other boys would make fun of country people. So he said nothing about where he came from, or who his family were, or why he hadn't been to that school before.

The bus blew exhaust fumes and dust about every time it stopped. And Grandpa tugged at Horace each time. "Is dis di stop?"

"No, Grandpa." Horace pulled away from him. He hoped that this new school would make him smart so he wouldn't grow up to be like Grandpa. He took his shoes off and shook out the dirt in them.

The buildings they passed were bigger, they had lots of windows, and cars were parked around them. Then Horace saw the big store where his mother had shopped in the week before school started, for pencils and a ruler, and his new lunch box.

"Next stop, Grandpa." Horace pushed passed the old man and ran down the aisle to the door. Then he heard a bell ring. He looked back at his grandfather to see the old man taking his hand off the bell cord before struggling to walk in time with the rocking motion of the bus.

Ashamed, Horace looked away. His grandfather did know about buses after all.

The store was even bigger than Horace remembered. It had counters everywhere and stairs to other floors, and people pushing this way and that. And nothing looked familiar. But he wouldn't tell Grandpa that.

"So a weh di boys clothes dem?" Grandpa asked no one in particular.

"Don't know, Grandpa."

Grandpa walked up to the nearest counter, pulling Horace with him. "A weh di boys' clothes dem, missis?" he asked the woman standing there. "Waan fit dis boy out fi school."

"At the back, sah. To di left."

"Come, boy." Grandpa put a hand firmly on his shoulder and guided him through the crowd, going toward the back of the store, and then to the left. The crowd was noisier here. The men pushed each other along the counters. They pushed Grandpa and Horace with them until they reached a doorway. The door led outside to the street.

"Is weh we is now?" Grandpa turned his lean head this way and that, looking about like a chicken at feeding time. They had made their way out of the store instead of to the back counter.

"But see yah," Grandpa chuckled. "Perhaps dem no waan sell us notten." He took hold of Horace's shoulder again. "Dis time we gwine reach."

They pushed through the other shoppers, burrowing their way along, one counter after another, to the back of the store. Boys clothing was across from yard goods in a dark corner. They couldn't see anyone serving there. Horace made a face. He smelt something sharp and acid, like chicken do-do, but not as stink. It made his eyes water and he didn't have anything to wipe his face.

"A weh di bell deh?" Grandpa searched between the piles of undershirts and handkerchiefs for the dome of the counter bell. Then he rapped on the worn counter top with his work-hardened knuckles. "Anybody bout yah?" he called out.

A curtain against the back wall moved. A petite black woman pulled the dull brown fabric aside. "Just one minute, sah."

"Yes, ma'am. When yuh ready, ma'am. Waan fit dis boy out fi school." Grandpa patted Horace on the head. He wished Grandpa would stop telling everyone why they were there.

"Patience, sir. It tek time fi a proper fitting." The woman's voice came from behind the curtain, firm and a little angry.

"Yes, ma'am, tek time, ma'am." Grandpa replied. Horace was afraid he would start chattering again.

When the woman came to serve them, she was short tempered with Grandpa. "Yuh don't know di boy's size? What yuh expect? Mi mus guess it?"

"Wait, nuh?" Grandpa waved at her as if dismissing her rudeness. "Mek we look on him shirt yah." He pulled up the boy's collar to show its label. "See it yah."

The woman looked at the label and mumbled, "Hum, next size must do." She made a pile, two sets of everything, shorts, shirts, socks, underwear, handkerchiefs. Then it was time for the cap. "What school?"

"Dis one." Horace pointed at the navy cloth school cap near the top of the display.

The woman sucked her teeth. She stooped behind the counter. The cap she took out was the wrong one.

"No ma'am," Horace said. "Dat one."

She made the rude noise again, put the cap back and brought out another. "Dis one?" She slapped the counter with it.

"Yes, ma'am."

"Good." She put the pile of clothes on to a sheet of brown paper, then wrote out a bill. She tore it off the pad and handed it to Grandpa. "Yuh pay over dere." She waved at the cashier, then started to wrap the parcel of clothes.

"Over so?" Grandpa asked.

"Yes, sah."

Grandpa didn't move. He watched the woman measure out string for the parcel.

She looked up. "Yuh mus pay fi it, ole man."

"Yes, ma'am. I did know dat."

"Now, man." Her voice got louder.

"What about di tings?"

"Yuh come back wid di bill mark 'paid' and den ah give it to yuh."

"Stay here." Grandpa said to Horace, who sighed loudly. He didn't want to follow his grandfather anyway. He didn't want to be next to him when he embarrassed himself again.

The boy and his grandfather came out onto the street. Horace took a deep breath and blinked to clear away the acid smell. His nose wrinkled at the scent of rotting fruit and animal droppings.

"I hungry. How bout yuh, boy?" Grandpa asked as he shifted the parcel under his arm.

"No. Mi waan go home." Horace headed for the bus stop.

"I did see one fine place fi eat from di bus. I tink is down so."

"Mi nuh waan go."

"Money leave from di dollars yuh madda give me. Mek we get someting wid it."

"Grandpa, I waan fi go home."

"And yuh mama want yuh out a di house." Grandpa tugged at Horace's sleeve. "So we going to eat at di fancy place down so."

"De fancy place" was a cafeteria. It looked new because it had big glass windows facing the street, and wasn't at all like the older buildings around it. They still had the old fashioned concrete columns and covered sidewalks, and small windows full of merchandise.

The cafeteria had shelves of pies, cakes and buns, and there were covered pots of soup, stews and rice. Grandpa stood in front of the display. "Look on dat, bwoy." The sweep of his arm included the whole selection. "What yuh want?"

"Dat yuh come out a mi way." A man carrying a tray of food tried to pass Grandpa.

"Dis way, Grandpa." Horace tugged at his grandfather's belt. "Yu start over so." He knew all about it. He was used to the cafeteria at school. But Grandpa didn't seem to understand what to do.

"Do yuh want one of dese?" Grandpa took a piece of pie from a shelf and put it on the tray the boy held. Then he reached for piece of cake. "Or maybe dis one taste sweeter."

"Dem don't like yuh to do dat." Horace wondered if he was getting used to Grandpa's way of doing things, because he was not upset anymore.

"Dem don't like what?"

"Yuh must tek just di one yuh want. Dem don't like yuh fi touch up di food." Horace took the cake from his grandfather's hand and set it on the tray.

They took glasses of orange juice and patties, and Grandpa paid the cashier. They sat at a table in one of the big windows. Horace watched the people walking by, the higglers selling on the sidewalk, the traffic on the street, and didn't pay any attention to Grandpa. When they had finished their lunch, they caught the bus home, and Grandpa managed to make the trip without looking foolish again.

In his new clothes, Horace felt he was just like the other boys at school. He particularly liked the way the cap made him look older. He wore it everywhere, except in the classroom, where the teachers reminded him to take it off.

He wore the cap into the school yard in the lunch break. One day the biggest boy in his class, Joseph Bramble, and his friends came up to him and asked him why he wore the cap.

"I like it," he answered.

"Like it, eh?" Joe Bramble reached out and grabbed the cap off his head and threw it to one of the others. The cap was tossed back and forth just out of Horace's reach.

"How yuh like it now?"

The cap had become crushed and misshapen with each boy's catch.

"Is alright." Horace put his hand out for it.

Joe Bramble had the cap. "Alright, country bwoy? Is alright, eh?" The school bell rang for the start of classes and he threw the cap high above his head. The other boys went into class, and Horace ran toward the falling cap. But he reached it too late to catch it. It kicked up a spit of dust as it hit the ground.

The next Sunday, Horace saw the boys coming down the street toward them just as he and his family were returning from church.

"Hey, country bwoy!" one of them called out.

"Dem is yuh little school friends?" his mother asked.

"Yes, Mama," he lied.

She took off her hat and went into their new concrete home. "Yuh father soon come looking fi lunch."

Grandpa sat on the wooden bench on the verandah. Horace tried to ignore the boys approaching the gate. But Grandpa called to him "Yuh not going say 'howdy' to yuh friends, bwoy?"

"Yes, Grandpa." Horace returned to the gate and

waved at the boys. They were just a few yards away now.

"Den yuh no wear yuh cap go church, country bwoy?" Joe Bramble called to him as the boys came up to the gate.

Horace went out into the street and talked quietly to them, hoping his grandfather wouldn't hear him. "Why yuh no leave me alone, and no come wid dis 'country bwoy' business here."

"Because yuh is a country bwoy," said Joe, as he slapped Horace on the cheek. "A country bwoy." He slapped the other side of his face.

"Yes, man." Someone struck him from behind. Another thumped his shoulder. Soon he could not tell where the blows came from; he just felt the pain and humiliation as they cried out, "Country bwoy," with each blow.

Suddenly these cries stopped, the beating stopped. Then: "No, man! Stop!" The boys protested and ran away. Horace looked up from where he had fallen. Grandpa stood over him with his cane raised. He brought it down on Joe Bramble's head.

"Coward! Leave di boy!" He whacked the bully again.

The other boys had already run off when Horace got up and reached out for his grandfather's cane. The old man let him take it from his grasp. Horace ran after Joe and caught him on the leg with one swing of the cane.

"Ah going get yuh, country bwoy," Joe called over his shoulder as he hurried after his friends, "when yuh no have dis ole man at yuh back, ah going get yuh."

Just as the boy and his grandfather opened their gate, a police cruiser turned into the street. An officer leaned out of the window: "What a go on yah?"

"Notten," Joe shouted back.

Horace froze at the gate, "Now it going mek it worse."

"No, no," Grandpa's hand was reassuring as it gently patted the boy's shoulder. "Is alright."

The car stopped at the gate. "Ole man, what happen yah?" the officer asked.

"Well, sah. Is like dis, sah." Grandpa turned from the gate and hobbled with the help of his cane to the bench on the verandah. He sat down slowly before he continued. "I did sit yah, pon di verandah, smoking one aishus staishus cigar, when I saw two ladies versiting."

"Ole man, is joke yuh joking wid mi now." The officer had got out of the car and was leaning on the gate. "Tell mi how it go, nuh man."

Grandpa smiled and winked at Horace. "These two lady versities was talking bout di commercities."

"Cho, is only foolishness yuh a talk." The officer got back into the car.

Horace watched the dust swirls that followed the car down the street. Then he climbed over the verandah wall to sit beside his grandfather. He watched his feet as he knocked dirt off his shoes.

"Yuh alright, bwoy?" Grandpa asked.

"Yes, sah." He looked up and saw the smile on his grandfather's face. He put out his hand, and Grandpa shook it as if he were a big man.

Green Bush

T he bell rang and Gillian started up the stairs to the art room, through the usual crush of boys juggling books and binders. She noticed that many of them were sitting on the stairs. The further up the steps she went, the more the boys lounged onto the stairs, grinning up at her as she passed. Suddenly it dawned on her - they were trying to see up her skirt. Gillian suppressed a smile. She paused, leaned over the banister and called out: "Pink flowers this morning, gentlemen."

The boys laughed and clapped; then their fun ended and they moved off to their classes. They didn't notice the man at the bottom of the steps who grinned up at Gillian and winked; nor the blush she tried to conceal by pulling her hair around her face. The tall, young teacher with the twinkling eyes was Rick Williams of the English Department. One lunch break in that first week he had come over and introduced himself with a, "How are things going?"

She hadn't gone into it at the time, but things weren't going well at all. Her husband Dan had just got

news about a transfer. It had been a possibility for so
long, they had stopped thinking about it. Now Dan's
company wanted them to move back to Canada within
a month. So, at home Gillian was up to her hips in boxes
and papers and packing. And her head ached with the
discussions (she avoided calling them arguments) caused
by her commitment to the school and to Dan's friend,
Tom.

One Thursday night, as they sat sipping gin and
tonic on the verandah, Dan's friend Tom had told them
about his plans to go abroad to paint. Gillian knew it
was a Thursday because, after Tom left, her husband
Dan made his usual Thursday night complaint about
his position at the bank... his I'm-not-paranoid-but
speech, she had come to call it.

She had tuned out and played back his college
friend's talk about his sabbatical plans. She began to
think it time she tried her hand at teaching again, that
the church school for boys would be a good place to start.
She hadn't used her teaching degree since Dan's transfer
to Kingston three years ago.

At first, moving into a pretty little bungalow, meeting
new people, and picnics on the Jamaican beaches had
brought a freshness to their marriage. Each weekend
they had followed nights of parties with lazy days of
suntanning by the sea. As the faces at the parties
became familiar, and the beaches lost the appeal of
discovery, so their relationship slipped back into the old
worn grooves; the same conversations, the same conflicts.
As the newness wore off, so did the veneer of peace.

Dan had begun to bring the worry he felt about his
work home to their bed. Gillian believed that her
temporary return to a career would provide a shift in
focus for her, and perhaps give her the patience to deal

with Dan. She decided to take Tom's place at the church school for the duration of his sabbatical.

She still felt guilty at her sense of relief at seeing Dan off at the airport. Maybe a couple of months apart was what they needed to take the sparks out of the conversations, and put them back into their lovemaking. She had closed up the bungalow and moved into a grimy, tackily furnished studio apartment near the school.

It had been a particularly warm day, the Saturday that Gillian had chosen to move into the apartment. She was unloading an armful of clothes and a bag of groceries from her car when she noticed a man in heavy workman's khaki sweeping the eaves of the building with an extra long handled broom. He was moving slowly, pushing the broom along the underside of the roof.

She took a tight grip on her possessions and headed for the stairs that led to her apartment. As she got closer to the man with the broom, she could see what he was doing. There was a cluster of wasps' nests clinging to the roof. The broom, under his guidance, was about to sweep them off the eaves.

With a firm push on the handle, the man brought down the nests. The broom clattered to the concrete walkway. The workman picked it up again and rubbed the bristles across the nests, destroying them. But when he checked his handiwork, angry wasps flew at him. He leapt off the pathway and ran toward the hibiscus hedge that bordered the carpark.

"Green bush, green bush", he cried out as he ran. He stopped by the hedge for a moment, his arms swatting at the wasps. "Green bush."

Then he backed away from the hedge and returned to his broom.

"Why 'green bush'?" asked Gillian.

"So dem will go in di bush an no trouble mi. Dat is how we get rid a di wasp dem."

Gillian left the bag of groceries on the kitchen counter and went to dump her clothes on the narrow bed in the corner of the apartment. She turned to the window. She was about to open the glass louvres to let some fresh air into the room, when she saw the wasp.

Crawling on the other side of the glass, it buzzed angrily, as if it wanted to be let in. She decided to leave the window closed for a little longer. Then she wondered if the man's mantra would work for her. "Green bush", she whispered. The wasp climbed further up the louvre. "Green bush", she said out loud. The wasp flew off the glass for a moment, but it came back to pitch on another louvre. "Green bush!" she shouted so loudly that she surprised herself. And then she started to laugh. It was a silly idea. She began to hang up clothes in the closet. A moment later, she checked the window. The wasp was gone.

The first few weeks had been difficult. Gillian had forgotten how awful early September can be, finding her way around a new set of classrooms, and organizing an art room with what was left of supplies someone else had ordered. Then there was the problem of matching names to the faces of staff and students.

By the third week, she had begun to feel she had things under control. But she soon discovered how wrong she was; that those boys, who looked so angelic singing at morning prayers, were just waiting for the right opportunity.

Gillian soon regretted her decision to try teaching again. One incident after another reminded her of why she had given it up before. She hated disciplining, yet she seemed to spend most of her day doing just that.

There was the afternoon when the class bully pulled a stool out from under Peewee Jones. The boy narrowly missed injury, much to the amusement of his classmates. Gillian had dealt with the bully in her own way of slowly tipping him and his chair on to the floor. Not exactly an ethical thing to do, but it did subdue the class. The bully managed to humiliate Peewee again the next week, by filling his mouth with red paint, then boxing him. He pushed Peewee to the front of the room for her to see the red liquid drooling down his trembling chin.

Gillian was telling Hanna, the librarian about these pranks when Rick came over to ask again how she was doing. His response to her could-be-better reply was an invitation to join him and their colleagues for a drink after work.

"I don't know," Gillian hesitated.

"Well, it is Friday, after all." he grinned. "Aw, come on."

So Gillian joined the Elbow-benders' Society, a group of her fellow teachers who met at a local pub for drinks every Friday after work. She and Rick became the most regular members of the "society", and were often the last to leave. At first she felt a little uneasy, even guilty, when she found herself alone with her young colleague. Why guilty she wasn't really sure. After all, her thoughts were all she had to keep her company in that dingy apartment. Now, not even a wasp buzzed around her place on the weekends. And it occurred to her that she had no way of knowing what Dan was up to in the house he had found for them in Canada. What was the harm if she was unfaithful in her mind.

Rick appeared to save Friday evenings for her. Drinks with the group would lead to one casual invitation after another. They seemed innocent enough, and that is how she chose to see their friendship. She enjoyed his attention and tried not to show her delight. But she seemed to have as much control over her feelings as she had over her students.

One morning she had spent fifteen minutes explaining the simple principles of stencil design to little Johnny Blomfeld. When she looked up she saw Harry Thompson slipping back into seat, his face wet, dripping on to his shirt. That's how she became aware that the sink at the back of the room was being used in a new way. Several of the class were testing how long they could hold their breath under water.

By the time she had reached this little group at the back, Jimmy Harvey had been distracted from his task as timer and had drawn the attention of the rest of the class to what he was watching: "Rahtid, look at dem titty deh!"

Gillian was forced to look out the window too. There, on the back porch of the old house next door, was a middle-aged woman hanging laundry onto a line. She seemed quite unaware of her appearance, her blouse only buttoned at her waist, and her ample bosom spilling out of an inadequate brassiere.

The giggling boys pressed their faces to the windows. Gillian returned to her desk and tried to restore order. "That's quite enough. Please return to your seats now."

The boys moved back to their places, still commenting crudely and laughing. She tried to settle them quickly. She said, "Gentlemen, every woman has two... so you shouldn't be surprised or laugh."

It worked, but not before the boys clapped and cheered, and not before she realized that Rick was standing at the classroom door. He gave a thumbs-up sign and moved away down the verandah. She wished she had learned not to blush easily, and she was relieved the boys ignored her as she shuffled papers on her desk.

Once she got over feeling embarrassed, her annoyance with Rick for being at the door watching her grew. What business was it of his, and what right did he have to put his nose into her classroom? Or was she over-reacting, making an issue out of a simple coincidence? But then, wasn't it indiscreet to be so friendly toward her, in front of the students?"

She was glad her students weren't around when the accident happened, even though they caused it. She had gone to the artroom after the lunch break to mark papers before her afternoon class. The door, which she was sure she had closed as usual, was slightly ajar. The room was as tidy as she had left if, except for the ceramics table. There, set neatly in a row, were the funnels she used when storing batik dyes. She went over to the table to pick them up and put them away. The funnels had been filled with plaster and had already set into shape.

She was checking to see what else they had done, taking a quick inventory of the items on the desk top, when Rick stuck his head through the door.

"Are you coming to have a drink with old Harris tonight? It's his birthday."

"Oh, I don't think so." And she was about to tell him about the plaster in the funnels when she sat on her chair and felt something give. The chair tipped suddenly to one side and would have deposited her on the floor if Rick hadn't caught her.

He pulled her to her feet and held her too long. He laughed, "Hey, I know you like me, but you don't have to throw yourself at my feet." He seemed reluctant to let her pull away. "But do you like me enough to stay like this?" The smile had gone from his face and he looked at her for an answer.

She turned to avoid reacting to him as much as to see what had happened to the chair. "Those damn kids!" She picked up a piece of wood. "Look! They sawed through it. God, this is the last straw!"

"A bit big for a straw, if you ask me." He reached out for the piece of chair leg, and stroked her fingers as they held it.

"What do you think you're doing?" she wanted to know.

"Taking things into my hands." He smiled and caught her, wrapping his fingers about the piece of chair leg.

Gillian jerked away, pulling the bit of wood out of his hand. "You've got some nerve."

Rick reached for her again. "What's wrong?" He frowned at her; he looked puzzled and angry. "Okay, that's it. I'm gone." And he walked out of the room.

Gillian moved the broken chair toward the door and set about preparing for her next class. When the bell rang, she sat at her desk and watched the boys file into the room.

Winston, one of the bigger boys, called his friends to see the broken chair by the door. They began to giggle and Barry, his sidekick, encouraged Winston to show them something else. Gillian watched the group of boys go to the back of the room to the table with the funnels. Winston pulled up one of the funnels, exposing the plaster. Barry tweaked the nipple-like point of the cone. The boys laughed so loudly they drew the attention of the rest of the class to their handiwork.

"That's enough," Gillian called, and she directed the boys to sit down. Then she called Barry and Winston to the front of the class. She handed them paper and charcoal pencils to pass out to the class. The two boys were about to sit down when she called them to the front of the room again.

"It's figure drawing today... and you'll be the models."

The boys grinned and posed in imitation of Michelangelo's David and Rodin's The Thinker. The class laughed with them. Then Gillian explained the positions she wanted them to assume. She said, "It's important to see the limbs in different positions in relation to each other and to the body to fully understand proportion."

Winston stood on one leg with his right arm over his head, his right hand grasping his left earlobe. His left hand held his knee close to his chest. Barry held his nose with one hand and his elbow with the other while he knelt on one knee beside his friend. Gillian was pleased with the effect she had achieved. The class laughed and jeered at the two boys.

"Is not funny, man," complained Winston. He wobbled, trying to balance on one leg.

"No," agreed Barry. "It hurt, man." He shifted his weight to his other knee, looked up and saw Gillian's frown and went back to his original pose.

"Plaster funnels and sawed chair legs aren't funny," she said.

The boys looked surprised, and then they nodded, understanding what she had done.

The bell rang to mark the end of the class. The students started to shuffle toward the door, chit-chatting, like the wasps on the eaves. Several boys stopped when they heard her laughing. "Green bush," she said. Then they buzzed out the door.

The Ace of Spades

It wasn't until that morning that I realized there must be something to a belief in Obeah, some kernel of truth among the ritual and superstition. Until that moment, when I found myself on that wet country road, staring in shock at my mud-splattered car, I had laughed at Obeah and its believers. I had scoffed at them for their remedies for every one of life's problems - *Oil of Don't Come Back* to be rid of a tiresome lover, and *Salt of Stay 'Weh* to keep remembered pain from returning. My scorn was fuelled by my ignorance and to some extent my fear.

But that morning, in the chill and damp of dawn, I listened to the soft bird calls echo in the sudden quiet and knew that underlying such naive nonsense were truths that I had not wanted to acknowledge before.

I silently asked Mavis to forgive me for my insensitivity. She had been our live-in maid in my teen years. Across the yard from the backdoor a barracks-like structure provided simple housing for this good-hearted woman and her aging mother. But Mavis believed that an evil spirit also dwelled there: "Di jumbie, it in deh, Miss Jean. It draw weh me bed from di wall. Every morning, I wake and di bed move right into di room."

I was old enough for her to confide in, and I thought, educated enough to know more about some things than she did: yet at that age I would neither judge her nor tell her secrets to my mother. But the jumbie, her poltergeist, was beyond my experience.

Mavis merely shrugged at my inability to help her. She went to the local Obeah-man for advice, and then to the small pharmacy on the market square to buy the *Oil of Gweh fi Good* recommended by the Obeah-man. She showed me the old Coca-cola bottle half full of green liquid, a dirty rag stuffed into the top as a stopper.

"Him say I mus sprinkle it pon di bed every night before I go to sleep. And di jumbie won't bodder me no more." And it must have worked, because Mavis never mentioned the ghost or her moving bed again.

As I grew older and supposedly wiser, I rationalized away Mavis' problem with moving furniture by using what I considered common sense and psychological reasoning. But on that early summer morning such sensible thinking seemed out of place. Besides, there was the evidence, one drab green Vauxhall liberally splattered with mud and loosened soil. The pattern of freshly dug sepia-red earth scattered across the front of the old car drew the eye to the bumper and the scar it had left in the embankment.

Mavis had refered to her jumbie as an agent of the devil. "Come to drive her to wickedness." She hadn't explained how that would be accomplished but the term "agent of the devil" had been familiar to me. It was a favourite of my high school principal, a portly, middle-aged woman given to lecturing loudly and at length on matters of discipline. But it was Mavis' interpretation of the phrase that I thought of that morning as I looked into the car at my travelling companion, Lydia. She was calmly retrieving those items in her bag that had been strewn about the backseat, stopping now and then to flip her long hair over her shoulder. It was a mish mash of things in her bag, carved masks with straw hair and bright eyes, brightly coloured cards with snake symbols on some and more otherworldly stuff I did not recognize. What was this woman into?

Lydia had dropped in unexpectedly to renew a brief acquaintance. I had met her while on holiday at a South American resort. And, as Lydia had reminded me, I had said, "If you should get to Jamaica, look me up." I came to regret that friendly impulse which had brought the young woman with the oversized knapsack to my door.

Lydia had arrived just before one of the few long weekends that I take off from my work. I had been looking forward for months to a restful visit with my friend Joanna in Negril. I called Joanna, but her reaction to Lydia's joining us was "the more, the merrier."

By setting out early on the Friday afternoon, we beat the worst of the weekend traffic which clogged the roads in Spanish Town and May Pen. The trucks of women going to market slowed the climb to Mandeville. For miles we watched plump women and baskets of produce bouncing about on makeshift benches in old, exhaust-belching trucks.

I passed the time trying to quiz Lydia on her plans, where she was coming from, and more importantly, where and when she was going. Lydia wasn't very forthcoming with answers, leaving odd gaps in her story. My focus was on the road so that, to me, her vagueness was just an impression rather than something specific.

We stopped for English-style high tea in the new

Manchester Hotel before making our way over the narrow, pothole-riddled road to Savanna-la-Mar. This time it was the drays, the market-bound, mule-drawn carts laden with plantains and yams that slowed our progress.

Dusk was darkening into night when we arrived at Joanna's bungalow near Negril. It was close enough for us to smell a hint of sea salt in the air, yet too far away to hear the sea's swish on sand.

Five hours of driving on narrow, poorly kept roads and I was ready for a quiet evening. But the others had different ideas. Joanna described the various men to be found at "a quaint little bar right on the beach", and Lydia enthusiastically hurried us out the door.

The bar was little more than a hut of wooden boards and thatch roofing. Its rum-barrel tables spilled out onto the sand. The place was obviously popular with tourists and locals, and with the skimpily-clad young women who seem to come with the furniture in such places. We sat at a table on the edge of the wooden floor, just far enough away from the reggae-blaring loudspeakers to allow for conversation.

"Crowd's not bad tonight," said Joanna. Then she leaned closer and pointed out a group at a table closer to the bar. "Those guys are always in here."

I looked at three men. The chains about their necks, exposed in the open fronts of their shirts, folded into the creases of their chests. "Landshark's corner?" I suggested.

No sooner said than one of them got up and came over to our table. His teeth shone white and false in his face as he smiled at us. "Could we buy you ladies a drink?" he asked.

"Thanks, but no. We just got ours." Joanna answered for all of us but Lydia's smile must have been encouraging.

He looked at her and bent his head toward her, saying, "Well, perhaps we could join you ladies and buy the next round." The smile disappeared from Lydia's face and she glared at him. "Didn't you hear my friend?" she asked, tossing her hair to one side.

"Well, now maybe I didn't," he said. He hesitated, then shrugged and turned to go back to his table.

"Hey, we can say no," Lydia called after him.

"Put a hex on him, did you?" Joanna laughed.

"You need something to ward off the evil spirits in here," I said.

Joanna laughed with us, but then she became defensive. "They're not such a bad bunch here. Not all of them are aging Lotharios."

Lydia was more impressed with the place than I. She kept drawing our attention away from the suntanned men at the bar to the odd bits and pieces hung on the walls and pillars. Chicken-feathered voodoo masks, and Mexican sugar-skulls were tucked into the fishnetting strung about in what must have started as an attempt at seaside decor.

"Actually, I think that's kind of neat," said Lydia. "You don't really notice them until you look closely... then there they are, these ghoulish things staring at me."

"Yeah, they're almost as goodlooking as the guys." My intolerant mood was showing.

"Aw, come on," Joanna protested. "Give 'em a break."

"I think we've given them enough of a break," I said. "There's no one interesting around. And, frankly, I'm too tired to care."

"You're right," Joanna touched my shoulder. "We should put this off until tomorrow."

"Party poopers," Lydia protested as we left the bar.

The next day the miles of Negril beach was covered

with tourists and the Saturday crowds. We gave up our search for sand and tried to get a tan lying on Joanna's poorly kept lawn. In the evening we ended up back at Bonzo's Bar, or whatever it was called. Not even the men in the corner bothered us this time, and Lydia's fascination for the Voodoo decor began to irritate me.

It was Lydia's whining about our quiet weekend at Sunday brunch that made me suggest that we drive over to Montego Bay to give her a glimpse of "Tourist Town". But we never made it to Mo Bay. Near Montpelier Joanna began to curse. She stopped her car at the side of the road and got out.

"Oh Jesus," she muttered. "We've got a flat tire."

"That's okay," said Lydia. "I can fix it." She looked as if she knew what she was doing, checking the spare and stomping on the wrench to loosen the lugs. "Easy when you know how," she grinned and flipped her hair over her shoulders.

Just as she started to fight with the jack, we heard a rustling noise in a nearby hedge. A stockily-built man in khaki work clothes came out on to the road. He was carrying a large digging fork and a spade balanced on his shoulder, and at first it looked as if he would walk past us without a word. But suddenly he stopped beside Lydia and said slowly and in a loud voice as if we were deaf, "Good day, ladies.

"Thank heavens," said Lydia, no longer concerned with her image of self-sufficiency. "Can you get this damn jack to work?"

"Can't go far wid yuh tire like dat, missus," the man said with authority.

"So we'd better fix it." Lydia cursed as she knelt beside the car again. She persevered with the jack while the man watched, nodding his approval every now and then before going on his way. When she had taken the flat tire off, she stood up. "There", she said, as she brushed dirt from her clothes.

"There what?" asked Joanna.

"I've done my bit," Lydia said. "You can just put on the spare now."

"Gee, thanks." Joanna and I knelt to the task, lifting the spare tire into place and tightening the lugs. It took so long to finish the job that we decided to give up on going to Montego Bay.

Monday was a holiday. And Negril beach was just as crowded as it had been on Saturday. By lunchtime, we had had enough of kicked sand and suntan oil, so, back in the cool of Joanna's kitchen, I suggested we make an early start for Kingston.

"What's the hurry?" Lydia asked.

"Yeah, why don't we try Bluefields Beach this afternoon?" Joanna suggested.

"Because I know Bluefields Beach. Half of Savanna-la-Mar ends up on that beach on a holiday." I really didn't want to drive back in the thick of the late holiday traffic.

"Why don't we go back first thing in the morning?" Lydia asked.

"'Cause I have to be at work in the morning," I replied.

"But you could get to work on time if we started out really early," Lydia said.

"And you'd miss all the traffic." Joanna joined her.

"We'd have to leave at some ungodly hour, like four o'clock," I protested.

"Hey, that would be great!" Lydia said. "We'd get to see the sunrise."

"At that hour of the morning, who cares about the sunrise?"

But when Joanna shrugged her shoulders and said, "It's up to you, Jean. But why don't you," I knew I had been out voted.

Bluefields Beach was even more crowded than Negril, with truck-loads of country folk splashing each other in the shallow water, and shouting at their squealing children. We bought guineps and mangoes from a street vendor and headed back to Joanna's front lawn. After supper, when my thumbs down dismissed her suggestion of another trip to Bonzo's Bar, Joanna brought out a pack of cards. The problem was what to play. Lydia was into bridge, I favoured canasta, and Joanna wanted to play poker. We had a go at all of them, but since we each knew little about the other's game, the lack of serious competition soon made the exercise as boring as going to the bar.

Lydia had the cards in her hands, shuffling them back and forth when she said, "I read cards sometimes." She said it quietly, so it was a moment before either of us picked up on it.

"Would you read mine?" Joanna asked.

"Sure."

She read our fortunes that night, using vague and mysterious terms: "You must make a choice - at the next crossroads in your life" and "There will be romance but you'll have to work to keep it." Such nonsense that neither of us took it seriously.

We didn't take her last trick seriously either. Just before we called it a night, she shuffled the pack and passed it around, asking each of us to take a card. Joanna was first, she drew the king of hearts.

"Romance imminent!" Lydia giggled.

Then I drew the jack of spades and Lydia frowned. She looked even more unhappy when she drew the ace of spades.

"Oh dear," she said, and put down the cards as if they were suddenly hot in her hands.

"What do you mean, 'oh dear'?" Joanna asked.

"Well, umm..." She obviously didn't want to tell us.

"Don't leave us hanging! Come on, what is it?" I asked.

"It's spades, they're bad luck."

"So we just won't invest in the stock market for a while," Joanna suggested.

"It's best if you don't think about it, anyway," said Lydia.

I didn't sleep too well that night. And four o'clock came too soon for me. But we packed up the car in minutes and set out for Kingston on a quiet empty road, just barely lit by dawn light. I tried to get Lydia to talk to keep me alert, but she soon dozed off and left me to hum some silly tune to keep myself awake.

When the sun came up, it looked like it would be a clear day, the pale blue skies were streaked with pinks and a soft breeze ruffled the greenery at the roadside. But as we started the climb to Mandeville, it clouded over and a light drizzle misted the windscreen as I turned the sharp curves of Spur Tree Hill. I yawned and kept thinking that it was downhill all the way from Mandeville, much easier going, and that we would make it to Kingston in good time.

The town was still asleep as I turned slowly through the square and out past the new hotel. I could tell that it had been raining harder here. The red earth had been washed from the embankments across the road in bright stripes. I slowed down, knowing how hazardous that slippery surface could be, especially with tires that weren't exactly thick with tread.

On the edge of town the road slopes to the right into a blind curve. It's a deceptive piece of highway; the slope is steeper than it appears. As I geared down a big dark shape turned the corner. It was a moment before I realized it was a truck, painted black. It looked larger than those colourful old Leylands usually found on these roads. The noise of its powerful engine filled the air as it ploughed up the hill toward me, its wide body taking up most of the road.

I instinctively knew the driver of this monster would not think to pull to one side for me and my Vauxhall. If I didn't find somewhere to put the car out of his way, he would drive right into us. I searched the embankment for an opening, and found one. The gap in the bank could be a road or a driveway. I started to brake, pumping and releasing to slow the car without skidding, but the tires wouldn't grip at all.

The car slipped on the greasy surface. I strained forward over the steering wheel, trying to see if the opening had a gate. I saw metal bars, but I couldn't tell if the gate was open enough to let the car through. My curse was loud enough to arouse Lydia. She cried out at the sight of the truck. Then she leaned over me to point at the gap in the embankment.

"Go in there!" she screamed in my ear as she pushed on the steering wheel.

The truck was almost on top of us. I tried to ignore Lydia's hand as I spun the wheel and the car swerved into the gap in the bank. As the truck roared past us, I slapped Lydia's hand out of my way and pulled the wheel the other way, turning the car back on to the road. But the slipping tires, the narrow gap and probably fate were against me. A "damn" escaped through my clenched teeth. I tugged on the wheel, but the car slid into the embankment. It hit with a loud thud, the front bumper gouging out the red earth that sprayed, thick and wet, all over the car.

For a moment, I stared at the earth-covered windscreen. A sick resentment rose as I sat there listening to the sudden silence. That was when I understood what Mavis meant by "an agent of the devil". I looked into the mirror that I'd just knocked askew, at Lydia reaching for her purse on the back seat, flipping her long hair over her shoulder.

Glossary

a - is, be am, are, it is, there, to, of, in, at
Ah - I
batty - backside, bottom
bodder - bother
bun - burn
cho - interjection of anger, impatience, disappointment
crocus - burlap, sacking, burlap bag, crocus bag
cyaan - can't
dat - that
deh - there
dem - them, also used to indicate plural (eg. di key dem the keys)
den - then
dere - there
di - the
dis - this
do-do - faeces
dose - those
dray - a roughly made wooden cart
duppy - ghost
Ee-Hee - Oh yes! Yes!
everyting - everything
fah - for
fi - for, to
ganja - marijuana
guzu - an act of obeah or witchcraft
gwan - go away
gwine - going to
haffi - have to
higgler - seller of small produce or goods

Jamaica white - local term for a person who looks white but is known by everybody in Jamaica to be slightly coloured.

Jeyes - a commom household disinfectant

jumbie - duppie, ghost

ku - look

Lawd - Lord

lef - leave, left

lickle - little

madda - mother

mass - mister, master

mawga - meagre, thin

mek - make

mi - I, me, my

missis - mistress

mus - must

no - not, an, is, are not, please, won't you

notten - nothing

nuff - enough

Obeah - the practice of malignant magic as widely known in Jamaica. The magic is designed or 'worked' upon or on behalf of someone, to be distinguished from Myal which is a curative or healing practice.

peeny wally - firefly

pickney - a young child

Poco - Pocomania, a religion mixing Christian fundamentalism with some African religious customs. Worship involves singing and dancing to drums, possession by ancestral and other spirits as well as Bible readings, prayer, testimony and sermon.

pon - at, upon, on

rahtid - a mild expletive

rass - the buttocks; often used in an exclamatory way to show strong opposition, scorn, anger.
sah - sir
seh - say
smaddy - somebody
someting - something
tek - take
tick - stick
tings - things
waan - want
wah - what
weh - which, what, whatever, where
wid - with
yah - here
yuh - you, yours

This Glossary contains Jamaican words and English words with non-standard usages as they appear in the text. The spellings and interpretation owe a great deal to the *Dictionary of Jamaican English* edited by F.G. Cassidy and R.B Lepage (Cambridge University Press, London, 1967, 1980).